The God Squad

The God Squad

(a spoof on the ex-gay movement)

Rik Isensee

Writer's Showcase presented by *Writer's Digest*
San Jose New York Lincoln Shanghai

The God Squad
(a spoof on the ex-gay movement)

All Rights Reserved © 2000 by Rik Isensee

No part of this book may be reproduced or transmitted in any form or by any means, graphic, electronic, or mechanical, including photocopying, recording, taping, or by any information storage or retrieval system, without the permission in writing from the publisher.

Published by Writer's Showcase presented by *Writer's Digest*
an imprint of iUniverse.com, Inc.

For information address:
iUniverse.com, Inc.
620 North 48th Street
Suite 201
Lincoln, NE 68504-3467
www.iuniverse.com

This is a work of fiction. Although it draws on various claims commonly made by ex-gay ministries and reparative therapists, any resemblance to an actual person, program, organization, or historical event is both unintentional and entirely coincidental.

ISBN: 0-595-00677-9

Printed in the United States of America

Epigraph

All God's creatures got a voice in the choir,
Some sing low, some sing higher
Some sing out loud on the telephone wire
Others clap their hands!

—Gospel Song

Contents

Epigraph v
Acknowledgments ix
1: God Save the Queens 1
2: Headed for Trouble 7
3: Escape 15
4: Homopathology 21
5: Pride Goeth before the Fall 27
6: Abominations 33
7: Petticoats and Pigskin 41
8: Exorcism 47
9: Cheesecake 53
10: Castro Scuffle 59
11: Here's Spit in Your Eye 63
12: What a Friend I've Found in Jesus 67
13: To the Street Called Straight 71
14: The Peter Meter 77
15: Fruit of the Loom 83
16: The Curse of Canaan 89
17: Dangerous Liaison 93

18: Precious Bodily Fluids 99
19: Walking Along the Precipice 105
20: Cyberspace Cadet 111
21: Into the Vortex 117
22: Amazing Grace 121
23: Face to Face 125
24: Reclaiming America 131
25: Walk Like a Man 137
26: David and Goliath 145
27: Jonathan and David 151
28: Passing the Love of Women 157
29: Homo Erectus 163
30: Hunky Punky 171
31: Stallion Ranch 177
32: Like a Virgin 181
33: Somebody's Gotta Do It 187
34: Beat the Devil 195
35: Sex, Lies, and Porno 199
36: Ye Shall Be as Gods 205
37: Dos Equis 209

Acknowledgments

I'd like to thank the psychotherapy clients I have worked with who were recovering from misguided attempts to cure them of their homosexuality. Although *The God Squad* is a send-up of ex-gay ministries, the actual experience of being torn between one's faith and one's sexuality can be excruciating. I have been impressed with the courage shown by many former ex-gays to speak the truth as they have known it, especially in the face of incredible pressure to see themselves as mentally ill, living in sin, and suffering from "sexual brokenness."

Thanks also to parishioners at Freedom In Christ Evangelical Church, a gay-positive ministry in San Francisco, who asked me to speak at their meeting. They shared with me some of their own personal experiences with ex-gay groups, as well as providing more gay-friendly interpretations of Scripture.

For background material, I am grateful to Sylvia Pennington for her book, *Ex-Gays? There Are None*; to Francine Rzeznik and Teodoro Maniaci, directors of the film One Nation Under God, for their thorough documentation of the ex-gay movement; and Jallen Rix, for sharing his workbook for recovery from ex-gay ministries, *Ex-Gay? No Way*.

Bible quotes in the text are from the Revised Standard Version; chapter 21 contains sections from Revelation; chapter 24 includes a pastiche of sermons by Jonathan Edwards. Although some events are exaggerated for comic effect, treatment modalities such as orgasmic reorientation, aversive therapy with electric shock, covert desensitization with nausea-inducing drugs, makeovers and sports, and even exorcism have been used by ex-gay ministries and reparative treatment programs in attempts to cure homosexuality. Some sexual exploitation of participants and suicidal attempts have also been documented by Sylvia Pennington and others.

This novel is dedicated to all former ex-gays in the hope that they may feel loved and honored exactly the way they are.

1: God Save the Queens

"Christians are not born—they are born again! We have to recruit."
—The Reverend Sly Slocock

Being on my knees was not an unfamiliar position. Even supplication and worship were not completely foreign concepts. What was new was being on the other side of the fence during the notorious Gay Pride March in San Francisco.

Escape, our ministry to ex-gays (or the God Squad, as we called ourselves) had set up by the barricade near the fountain at United Nations Plaza, just as the parade entered the rally already in full swing at the Civic Center. The Reverend Sly Slocock gathered us around him in a circle on our knees, his hands raised in benediction. "Oh Lord, fill us with thy bounteous Mercy here at the very seat of Sodom. Grant us the strength to bear witness to your Redemption, guide us from Temptation, and deliver us from Evil." He pronounced Evil as though it had three syllables: Ee-vee-yil. Then he pulled us to our feet and we bent over in a football huddle. "He's the One! He's the Way! One Way for Jesus!" We clasped hands in the center and shouted "Yo!" then pointed our index fingers toward heaven.

We picked up our signs and fell in line. Sly held up the old standby, "Adam and Eve, not Adam and Steve!" Ruth, Sly's younger sister, picked "Directions to Heaven—Turn Right, Go Straight!" Jackson waved "Avert your eyes from Sodom!" and Perry took "Gird thy loins for Spiritual Warfare!" I never understood exactly where the loins are, though I'm sure we were all sufficiently girded, in contrast to the half-naked demonstrators swaggering before us.

Sheila, our resident recovering lesbian, held "Feminine, not Feminist!" This despite the fact that she had a Dutch-boy haircut and wore a leather jacket over her tanktop. To accommodate Ruth's attempts to make her over, Sheila wore ruby lipstick and applied some blush. Given her pale complexion, the rosy circles on her cheeks gave her a slightly clownish appearance, but we were all doing the best we could.

Then there was mine, my personal favorite: "Hell hath no fury like a Queen Re-Born!" This sign had required special permission from the Rev, who needed some convincing that it reflected the proper tone.

We waved our signs, bouncing on our feet, and chanted in unison: "God save the Queens! God save the Queens! God save the Queens!"

I liked our group because it had a certain flare, unlike our humorless rivals parked on the other side of Market. Wearing sleeveless sweatshirts and swigging beers, they held signs like "God Hates Queers," "Faggots Suck!" "Suffer Not a Sodomite to Live!" "Repent or Perish!" and "Stone a Homo, Go to Heaven." Just the sort of negative tactic that frightens gays away from true Salvation. Our God is a compassionate God—he hates the sin, but loves the sinner.

I suspect our spunk had something to do with the fact that most of us had at one time been practicing homosexuals (and many had, in fact, become quite good at it). Not that anyone's born that way, but we've retained a dash of spice in our style of demonstrating, despite the Rev's dark prophecies.

Reverend Slocock believed we were in the Final Days—the Time of Troubles with False Prophets everywhere: New Age heretics, witches and pagans, mediums and spiritualists of every stripe hawking their wares in the supermarket of the Soul. He was convinced the new Millennium would bring the final Rapture. I gazed across the sea of men passing by us and for a moment felt overwhelmed by our Herculean task. So many souls, so little time.

After weeks of preparation, this was our first foray into the secular world, witnessing for Jesus. Our mission was to recruit gays who had grown disillusioned with the lifestyle, just as many of us had. But so many disenchanted gays had no idea where to turn. Escape finally offered a genuine choice: sodomy and degradation, or Eternal Paradise.

Sly curled his lip at our queeny chant, then broke into a harsh rendition of "A Mighty Fortress is Our God, a Bulwark Never Failing." The rest of us joined in, discretely at first, but then the vigor of his war-whoop spurred us on to the next song. We joined hands above our heads as our voices rang out: "Onward Christian soldiers, marching as to war, with the Cross of Jesus, going on before!" In contrast to my previous history, this time my throat opened wide in service to the Lord, singing His praises. We marched in step and waved our signs to the military tempo.

The Rev pulled out his camcorder and handed it to Ruth, who got a shot of him and his running commentary as one festive float after another paraded by the reviewing stand. He's working on the next edition of his video, "The Homosexual Conspiracy," which he uses as a fundraiser for Escape. He's been to every parade for the last fifteen years, then edits the most outrageous footage he can find to expose the covert gay agenda for what it really is: a Satanic Plot to undermine the American Family.

He started off with his usual viewer warning: "Here we are at the so-called Gay Freedom Day Parade. The following footage may contain material that is unsuitable for ladies and children, as many of these perverted souls flaunt their lustful indecency in the face of the crowds and cameras.

"Behind us you see a float from a bar called the Stud: a truckload of half-drunk, barely clad youths hanging on each other, swigging beer, gyrating their hips to a raucous rendition of Aretha Franklin's "Respect" blaring from the loudspeaker. The irony of this exhibition is too obvious for comment. Following the Stud, we see a drumming, clattering band of Amazonian women banging on sticks and skins and bells, whooping and hollering like jungle birds. The racket is deafening.

"Next comes a group of the most grotesque-looking figures—men dressed as nuns, my God how disgusting, with white-face and ruby lips protruding from beards framed by starched, stiff habits. Their satin banner proclaims their decadence in Gothic letters: 'Sisters of Perpetual Indulgence.' How these purveyors of perversion gloat and swagger with carnal desire 'in such a time as this!'"

The Rev always commented on everything that passed in front of the camera to make sure the viewer understood the full extent of the depravity he was witnessing.

"Here come the Radical Fairies," he continued, "typical of these queer folk—like the cast from Dante's Inferno, if you ask me—elves, fairies, and queens, looking quite childlike at first, until you notice the bare bottoms, the cloven hooves, Pan's horns, and the deviltry incarnate in the pagan procession parading before us."

One peculiar fellow, naked except for a satyr's phallus strapped to his groin, wore a devil's mask and bat-like wings, a scarlet cape emblazoned with "Jesus Christ Satan" trailing behind him. This really got Sly's goat. "How brazenly blasphemous! What sacrilege they allow in the streets of San Francisco! Look how he prances about cracking a whip at the crowd. See how they coo and crow with bestial pleasure!"

Sly took the camera from Ruth and zoomed in on a more militant group just ccoming into view. Mostly men, they wore black T-shirts with pink triangles proclaiming DEFIANCE = DEPTH. They carried an ACT-OUT banner from the AIDS Coalition To Outrage Unsuspecting Tourists, shaking their fists, chanting "Act out, fight back, fight AIDS!"

A shrill whistle pierced the air and suddenly everyone fell stricken to the ground, a pool of blood-like fluid spilled across the asphalt. The few left standing hurriedly drew chalk lines around the fallen bodies. A man with a loudspeaker rattled off statistics of daily AIDS deaths. Then they sprang to their feet again, chanting their slogan.

A group of younger guys followed closely behind, carrying a HOMO NATION banner. Many wore baseball caps turned backwards, baggy shorts and combat boots, some with leather jackets emblazoned with day-glo stickers: IN YOUR FACE and LOVE IT OR LICK IT. One carried a placard that read: POLYESTER BLENDS ARE AN ABOMINATION!—Leviticus, 19:19, and another held up NO SPECIAL RIGHTS FOR THE RELIGIOUS RIGHT! Passing by the reviewing stand, they shouted:

We're Homo,
We're PoMo,
And we ain't gonna take it
No Mo'!

A bunch of cops wearing surgical masks and yellow gloves had lined up alongside the barricades in response to Act-Out's die-in. The demonstrators snapped their fingers at the cops and sang, "No matter what you say or do, your gloves don't match your shoes!"

Passing our group, they turned their angry faces toward us and pointed at our signs. "Shame! Shame! Shame!" they chanted. Sly looked up from his camera and shook his head at the sad irony of it all. "How oblivious they are of the Truth that could save them from the everlasting suffering that makes our worldly pain pale by comparison," he declared.

I couldn't agree more. Yet as they marched by, shouting and pointing, I almost admired their brazenness. One guy with dark eyebrows knitted in a fierce scowl, his cheeks rosy in the cool wind, his lips full of blood, made eye contact with me for a brief moment. Watching his smooth muscles tighten beneath his black T-shirt as he shouted "Shame!" and thrust his fist in the air, I had a sudden inspiration.

"Jesus loves you!" I yelled.

"Fuck you!" he shot back, glaring directly at me. Then everyone around him gave us the finger as they picked up the chant: "Fuck you! Fuck you! Fuck you!"

My face went hot, as though I'd been slapped; yet I felt a wrenching in my heart with the sense that this anguished soul had established an instant connection with me. No matter that he spurned my entreaty, scorned God—that's expectable. I had spoken to him; he heard me, and responded.

Sly was in heaven. "This is such great footage." He kept the camera whirring as they strutted past us.

The fellow I'd made contact with kept shouting "Fuck you!" as he shoved his obscene gesture in the air. I had an impulse to run after him and try to turn him from his sinful ways, but I lost sight of him as the boys from Homo Nation dispersed into Civic Center Plaza. Sly put the camera down to his side. "How juvenile and pathetic," he said, "and how lost."

I nodded. To think that at one point I might have counted myself among them, perish the thought.

Ruth said, "Good for you, Paul," and squeezed my hand.

For some reason, I shuddered.

2: Headed for Trouble

I wasn't always a Jesus freak. My salvation came at the end of a long road of dissolute living—you know, the usual suspects: drugs, sex, and rock and roll.

I was a rebel—against what I didn't know—perhaps the boredom of a permissive, anything goes sort of family. My parents were hip—they smoked dope, had long hair, wore Birkenstocks. I grew up listening to the Grateful Dead and Madonna. My parents had a portrait of some guru called Mayor Baba over the fireplace. He peered out at us with a moustache and a stoned-looking grin, his mantra inscribed beneath his chin: "Don't worry, be happy!" I can't imagine a town that would elect a mayor with such a lame slogan. As if anything worthwhile was ever that easy.

They finally got married when I was four, only because they thought they'd get a better tax break (another mistake). I still have a photo of us in a meadow surrounded by redwoods, deep in the Santa Cruz mountains. My father had a beard and long hair. He wore bell bottoms with a white peasant shirt open to the middle of his chest with a long necklace of acorns and squash seeds. My mother wore a dress made out of an Indian bedspread and a garland of flowers on top of her braided hair. A boombox played "You Are the Sunshine of My Life" by Stevie Wonder, while guests dressed in folk costumes danced around a May pole.

I was the ring bearer. They dressed me like a forest sprite in leafy vines that turned out to be poison oak. I was hospitalized for a week while they went off to see Mayor Baba for their honeymoon. They arrived in India only to discover that Baba had dropped his body some years before. Oh well.

We lived in a commune in Oakland based on the principles of Summerhill, this kooky experimental school in England: children will naturally develop consideration for others if they are raised with consideration for them. In the meantime, you're supposed to put up with whatever the little bastards did to you.

By the time I was six, my father had long since taken off to "find" himself. After traveling to Thailand and Indonesia, he eventually found himself with a much younger version of my mother, a hippie maiden he met in Bali who worked with the Santa Cruz Food Conspiracy.

After my father abandoned us, my mother underwent a change from earth mother to feminist. We moved into an apartment by ourselves in Berkeley, which was a big relief. At least I no longer had to share a bedroom with Moonbeam, Stargaze, and Sunsprout. She got a job at the Women's Health Collective, cut her hair, got rid of the Indian bedspreads, and replaced the portrait of Mayor Baba with Emma Goldman. She even stopped smoking dope, although she still "dabbled" in coke.

She wouldn't let me watch TV because of all the sexist violence and exploitive ads. I had to sneak over to a friend's house to see Sesame Street. I could never keep up with the latest shoes, jeans, or underwear. When it came to the Superbowl or the World Series, I never knew whether it was football, baseball, or basketball, much less which side we were on. This put me at a distinct disadvantage among my classmates, whose reality seemed more defined by what they saw on TV than by what we did with each other. Which I suppose is what my mother objected to, but I felt deprived and out of it.

In junior high, I wanted to join the Boy Scouts, but my mom said they were run by a bunch of paramilitary fascists, and she objected to my wearing a uniform. I insisted on joining despite her disapproval. I liked wearing a uniform and getting those nifty merit badges, going on campouts, telling ghost stories, and singing around the campfire.

In the midst of our songfest, our Scoutmaster would suddenly leap out of his tent wearing nothing but underpants and a towel wrapped around his forehead, which draped down the back of his neck. Then he'd sing, "I am the Sheik of Araby—"

And we'd all shout: "With no pants on!"

"Each night I start to creep—"

"With no pants on!"

"Around the camp I'll sneak—"

"With no pants on!"

"And into your tent I'll peek!"

"With no pants on!"

Then he'd reach out his gangly arms and try to tickle us. We'd all shriek with laughter, especially at the sight of Mr. Jenks, who was normally so strict and uptight, running around in his BVDs.

Late at night, after he'd gone to bed, we'd huddle in our tents and tell dirty jokes, then peer inside each other's sleeping bags with our flashlights to see who was getting hair.

At our weekly meetings, I loved tying knots. I soon learned the difference between a square knot and a "granny" (right over left, left over right). I always volunteered when Matt, our Junior Assistant Scoutmaster, demonstrated the bowline. The bowline is a great knot to know if you're caught on a ledge, 'cause you can tie it around your waist with one hand while you hold onto the rope with the other. Then your buddies just pull you up the cliff.

Matt was seventeen. He wore the forest green uniform of Explorer Scouts, which looked a lot swifter than our drab olive khakis. He'd wrap his arms around my waist and tie the bowline in front of me while I stood cradled in his arms, smelling his English Leather aftershave.

One night after a meeting, my Mom came by to pick me up and found us holding hands in our closing circle. I always made sure I stood next to Matt. We bowed our heads while Mr. Jenks intoned "May the Great

Scoutmaster, over all Scouts, be with us till we meet again." Matt squeezed my hand and said, "Goodnight, Scouts!"

Mom told the Scoutmaster we were Buddhists and she objected to sectarian observances. Unfortunately, Mr. Jenks was not into multiculturalism, so he threw me out for being an atheist. That was the end of Boy Scouts.

Mom always said I should think for myself, but what did I know—I was only a dumb kid. After getting kicked out of the Boy Scouts, I was aimless, looking for direction, yearning for answers. I was no good at athletics, a nerd without a computer, a total fumbler when it came to girls. Mom had warned me not to take advantage—"I did not raise my son to be a rapist," she always said—but I never knew what girls expected of me. I figured it was up to them to make the first move. Not being as liberated as my mother, of course they never did; so on the rare occasion when I actually took a girl out on a date, nothing happened. Which was kind of a relief, to tell you the truth.

Not knowing which way to turn, I dropped out of school and fell into a bad crowd—minor scrapes with the law for truancy, grafitti, and joy-riding. I smoked dope, hung out in dirty book stores, under the pier or the railroad trestle, ready for a wank. I thought I was such a smart ass, a bad dude, but I was just a young punk headed for Trouble.

One night my mom got called to pick me up from Juvenile Hall for stealing some porn magazines from a cigar store on Telegraph Avenue. She tried to have a Talk with me while she drove me home in the rain.

"Ever since your father left, I've never been sure whether I was doing the right thing by you. Maybe you needed a man, a role model, someone you could look up to—"

"You were the one who yanked me out of Scouting."

"I never took you out of the Boy Scouts. They persecuted you for not being a Christian."

"Oh, right. After you insisted we were atheists so I couldn't pray with them."

"I never said we were atheists, I said we were Buddhists."

"Same thing." She might as well have told them we were Hare Krishnas from the Temple of Doom, for all my Scoutmaster knew.

"I just don't understand what's gotten into you. You were always such a thoughtful boy, considerate and kind—"

"Don't forget obedient, cheerful, thrifty, brave, clean and reverent."

She looked annoyed, as she usually did with my sarcasm. But she refused to take the bait.

"Or what about physically strong, mentally awake, and morally straight?" I had to rub it in.

After a pause she said, "Paul, tell me. Do you think you might be…gay?"

I folded my arms across my chest, and stared at the rain splashing against the windshield. The cops obviously showed her the magazines, the bastards. "The kid's queer, lady. You better get him some help."

"Because if you are, it's really okay."

I'd honestly have felt better if she'd been horrified and taken me right to a priest to have me exorcised, except I'd never once in my whole life even stepped inside a church. Or at least to a shrink. I just couldn't accept her being so agreeable, given how much I was already condemning myself. Although at that point I was hell-bent on rebelling against her no matter what she suggested. I was just that ornery.

"You know, there's a gay bookstore over in San Francisco. We could go over there and maybe you'll find something you'd like to read."

"Oh brother." Like I could just see going into some homo bookstore with my mother.

"I'm just, you know, concerned. About AIDS and all. Plus you don't have to steal those magazines. I'm perfectly willing—"

"Mother, would you just drop it?"

"Paul, I am just trying to be helpful."

"Well I don't need any of your stupid help."

I expected her to get that wounded look like she does when I've said about the worst thing ever to hurt her feelings. I was determined not to buy into it.

Instead, she slammed on the brakes and the car swerved to a halt on the wet asphalt. She turned toward me with that look in her eyes that always meant business. "Look, buster, if you don't need my 'stupid help,' you can damn well walk home."

"Mom—"

"Who just rescued your scrawny butt from Juvenile Hall for some juvenile prank?"

I curled my upper lip in disdain.

"Get out," she said, and pushed my shoulder.

"It's raining."

"So get soaked, you snotty brat."

I refused to budge. She turned off the ignition. "We'll just sit here, then."

"Mom, come on."

"We are not going anywhere until you apologize!"

"Okay. I'm sorry," I said, but she sat there, fuming. "So can we just go?"

"Not until you say it like you mean it."

"I said I was sorry! What do you want me to do, go down on my goddam knees?"

"Get out."

I grabbed the keys and jumped out of the car, dangling them in front of the windshield. She chased me a few yards while I hopped around in the rain, jingling the keys, and darted out of her way, laughing like a nutcase. "Mom! I am so sorry! You'll never believe how incredibly sorry I am."

She stopped chasing me and crossed her arms, furious. Her hair blew in flat wet ribbons across her face.

"Mom! I swear I have never in my life been so utterly, absolutely sorry as I am at this very moment." I held up three fingers. "Scout's honor. Can you ever forgive me?" She glared at me. "Pretty please, with honey and sugar? Oh, I forgot," I giggled, clutching my side, "we don't do sugar. Pretty please with honey and just a 'dabble' of coke?"

"You little bastard!" She thrust out her hand, her bangle bracelets clanging. "Give me those keys, right this instant!"

"Fuck you." I drew back my arm and heaved them across the road. We heard a squishy plop as they dropped into the slough. Oops. I didn't mean to toss them quite that far.

Her eyes flaming, her nostrils flared, she let out a blood-curdling stream of curses. Lunging at me, she looked like Mother Kali, the devouring goddess from Hindu mythology she had pasted on the refrigerator door. With a ferocious glare and human skulls wrapped in a necklace around her neck, she always gave me the shivers. I side-stepped her twice, then decided the better part of valor would be to hightail it home.

*　　*　　*

After our little incident I made myself scarce. In anticipation of leaving home, I secretly sold off her record collection from the 'seventies. Once I turned eighteen, I hitched to San Francisco and got a room in a seedy hotel in the Tenderloin. I hung out on Polk Street and snuck into rave clubs like Rage, Fracas, and Fiend. Over the next few months, I partied till I ran out of money and got thrown out of the hotel. Then I sold some dope, got hooked on speed, and before I realized it, started down that slippery slope toward Sodom.

Late one terminally dismal night, after being slipped a mickey and robbed by a guy I thought was a hot date, I staggered down Polk Street and collapsed in the gutter. I was twitching and tweaking like a maniac, when this van pulled up to the curb. The passenger door swung open and a gruff voice said, "Get in."

He no doubt thought I was a hustler, although I couldn't imagine what he wanted with me in my present condition. I never thought I would stoop so low that I'd be willing to peddle my ass. But at this point I was so miserable and desperate, I figured if some geezer gets off giving a wank to a boy covered with gutter muck, what the hell difference does it make? At least I'd get a shower and maybe a meal out of it.

I was jittery, freezing, and starving. I got up on my knees and leaned on the front seat. The driver grabbed me by the scruff of my neck and yanked me into the van. I looked up to discover a square-jawed man with a gray crewcut in his fifties. He wore camouflage fatigues and a flak jacket with a clerical collar. "I'm the Reverend Sly Slocock," he said, "and your ass has just been saved."

By the grace of God, instead of being dumped off Pier 39 in a garbage bag, I was delivered into Salvation.

3: Escape

Fanatics always held a certain fascination for me. They seemed so sure of themselves, whereas I wasn't sure of anything. In order for them to be so convinced of the truth, I figured they must know something I didn't. I was attracted to their certainty, their righteousness, and the purity of their faith.

Most of my life, I'd felt left out, hesitant, confused. Here was a group of people who had found Salvation and who knew right from wrong. None of this relativistic, anything goes kind of morality. Even knowing where I'd been, they welcomed me and cherished me, and genuinely wanted me to be part of them. I responded immediately to their love and caring; besides, I needed a place to stay.

The residents and counselors of Escape lived in a safe-house in Chagrin County, as the Reverend liked to call it, just north of San Francisco. The grounds consisted of an old ranch house with a few out buildings nestled against a hill near Mt. Tam. I arrived shortly after a few other recruits, and we got our orientation to the program the next morning.

I entered this musty old barn that had been converted into an auditorium with a screen backdrop on the stage. It took a moment for my eyes to adjust to the dim light. Sheila, dressed in a sweatshirt and jeans, was already seated in one of the folding chairs, her foot tapping on the seat in front of her.

Perry sat quietly with his hands folded in his lap. He looked about sixteen, and wore a polo shirt and slacks, his hair freshly combed. I came in and sat a couple of chairs away from him. I said "Hi."

He said "Hi," then looked away, blushing.

Jackson came in wearing a loose Oakland A's T-shirt, the waist of his baggy shorts worn low, showing his underwear, his high-top athletic shoes untied. He took one look at me and put his hand to the side of his face. "Miss Thing!" he exclaimed.

Then he took a seat next to Sheila. He whispered something to her and giggled. She shrugged him off.

Sly had filled me in about the other residents the night before as we crossed the Golden Gate Bridge. He got his recruits, or "boots," as he called us, from various sources. Perry's very serious and pious, but his parents contacted Sly after they caught him with a neighbor boy. Jackson, a swishy black youth, escaped from Oakland when his parents threw him out on the street. Sly found him bruised and battered next to a dumpster in the Tenderloin, wearing a dress. "Some sailor picked him up in a tranny bar and got the surprise of his life when he reached between his legs," he said. Ruth nursed Jackson back to health.

Sheila, on the other hand, has a hard time being femme. She joined Escape after leaving an abusive relationship with a butch lesbian. "She throws a mean curveball and knows karate," Sly said, "but we don't let her play sports with the boys. Ruth keeps making her over so she'll look more demure, but in no time at all her bows are askew and her hair looks like something the cat dragged in. She's a twenty-three year old tomboy." Sly shook his head.

Even though there were only four of us in the audience, the Rev got up on the stage and lectured from the podium. "Welcome to Escape. You have taken a significant step on the road toward sexual wholeness. Let's give yourselves a big hand." All four of us clapped.

"Every part of the day has a function in your sexual, moral, and spiritual rehabilitation," he continued. "You'll have a daily routine, which consists of morning prayers, chores, and breakfast; an occasional lecture by Ruth, treatment for sexual brokenness, and lunch; clean up, Bible study, vigorous sports and cold showers for the men, and makeovers for the girls, followed by supper; then fellowshipping, evening vespers, and finally, after a busy, productive day, off to bed. As you can see, you have embarked on a rigorous program. It's a lot to keep track of, but you'll get up to speed soon enough."

We all sat there with blank expressions. I myself was a little stunned by the comprehensive nature of our treatment. It was no summer camp I'd signed up for.

Sly smiled. "Please, please, don't look so dour. This is serious business, but salvation can be fun! We will worship together and play together, and lift our voices to Empyrean Heights!"

Here he introduced his partner, a rather severe-looking woman in her late thirties, who joined him at the lectern. "This is Ruth, my sister in the flesh as well as in the spirit."

Ruth wore a dumpy black dress, her hair pulled back in a tight bun, and peered out at us through thick glasses. "Do you know what 'Escape' stands for?" she asked.

We shook our heads.

"Escape stands for 'Ex-gays Saved by Charismatic Apotheosis Prior to Eternity,'" she said. I thought this was quite a mouthful, and wasn't entirely sure what it meant, but it sounded impressive.

"Escape is generously provided for those who desire recovery from sexual brokenness. Unfortunately, ever since the removal of homosexuality from the list of mental disorders—because of the unrelenting political pressure brought to bear by the homosexual lobby—we have been unable to get reimbursement for treatment of the homosexual condition. Despite the opposition by the well-heeled homosexual establishment, I just wanted to announce that we have applied for a government grant to establish a research clinic on Reparative Therapy." We all clapped, and Ruth curtsied. "Until the grant comes through, we ask no money, only a little of your time outside of your studies, therapy, and prayers to help out with the water filter concessions." Ruth took her seat, and the Rev stepped up to the podium.

"I'll explain more about the filter business in a minute. But first, let me offer a little testimonial to introduce myself and our ministry. You may be wondering how a scruffy vet like me ended up wearing one of these." He tugged at his clerical collar, which poked out of his camouflage shirt and made his sun-burnt neck look like raw meat.

"While still in Nam, I slipped into heroin and diddled in homosexuality. I admit that I was lonely in country, and the comforting touch of a comrade in arms tempted me. When we abandoned that pitiful hellhole to its Communist fate, I descended into a self-made hell that made the war seem like a birthday party— brawling in bars, shooting up speed, heroin, and anything I could get my hands on. I was caught in an endless downward spiral of raunchy homosex, drugs, and degradation. I finally hit bottom and made my break through Synanon, by the grace of our Lord and Saviour, Jesus Christ.

"Of course there's not much money in religion, so I became a computer freak, a video-maker, and inventor. I am what's known in the trade as an autodidact—a self-taught man, member of Mensa, tip of the top one-tenth of one percent intelligence on this planet, if I do say so myself, with all modesty, of course. I invented the Crystal Spring Water Filter." He held up a silver cylinder with a tiny hose attached to its base, a small faucet extending from the top. "That's what currently brings in the bacon, but I've got other plans for combining computer technology with video imaging, which you will all see in due time."

I leaned over to Jackson to ask him if he'd seen any of these computer-enhanced video images, but he shook his head. "Just the videos he made of the gay parades," he whispered. "We oughtta take a look sometime. They're hot."

I looked back at him, a little surprised, while Sly continued his lecture: "Water is the principle compound in all the precious bodily fluids: blood, sweat, and tears, and of course, semen. Unfortunately, the Communist-inspired pseudo-scientific cabal has conspired to pollute the precious waters with the base element, fluoride!"

Ruth, seated off to the side, nodded sagely.

"Do you know what fluoride does to a man?" he demanded.

We shook our heads. I thought it just kept us from getting cavities, but soon learned this was a naive notion.

"Since they started poisoning our wells with that malignant toxin, the sperm count in the average male has fallen by fifty percent! Fifty percent, in the last fifty years! At that rate, the human race will be completely wiped out by the middle of the twenty-first century!

"I invented a reverse osmosis filter which removes the fluoride and organic residues from unclean farming practices. We sell these filters to support Escape's Reparative Program. You'll be working the water filter concessions at our store here on campus, and when you're ready to fledge, at the street fairs." He put the filter inside the podium, and folded his hands on top.

"Here at Escape, there are very few rules; but the rules we have are extremely important. They were devised over many years of healing practice in order to help you cleave to the straight and narrow path, lest you falter and fling yourselves unwittingly into the abyss.

"Rule number one: Don't read any homosexual propaganda, or anything from the pro-gay media. If the TV shows homosexuals in a favorable light, turn it off. Rule number two: Don't associate with anyone who advocates the gay lifestyle. Rule number three: Avoid temptation. If a good-looking guy comes into the store, get Ruth or Sheila to wait on him. And last, but not least, don't ever go to San Francisco by yourself!

"We're in the end times, folks, the Final Days, the new Millennium. And remember, Chagrin County is a hotbed of New Age heretics and allotheism—the worship of strange gods. Beware the Mark of the Beast: 666. 'Do not turn to mediums or wizards; do not seek them out, to be defiled by them…a medium or wizard shall be put to death; they shall be stoned with stones, their blood shall be upon them.'

"For that matter, don't go to places where non-Christians hang out, and don't read any non-Christian books. And for the sake of heaven, don't allow anyone to read your palm, throw the I Ching, or do your Tarot. The occult is from Satan!

"Welcome, campers! You'll have a little break before Ruth's lecture, so be back here by 10:15, sharp."

We got up and stretched. "Oh man!" Jackson whined. "We gonna sit in them hard chairs for a whole other hour? My booty been dented!" he walked outside rubbing his butt. Perry squinted in the bright sunlight.

This seemed like a pretty together organization to me. I liked structure and routines. I only hoped I was up to all the demands that would be placed on me. I leaned against the doorway and watched Sheila and Jackson play with a hackey sack. Sheila hit it off the inside of her shoe, lobbing it over to Jackson who bounced it off his heel, spun around and knocked it with his elbow, then off his knee back to Sheila. Ruth walked by with a scowl expressing her obvious disapproval. Sheila stuck out her tongue out as soon as Ruth's back was turned, and kept playing with Jackson.

Perry, looking pensive, strolled by himself across the grounds, which consisted of rose beds and a couple of live oak trees between the main building and the bunkhouse. A playing field extended all the way to the woods, and my heart sank at the thought of running around the tightly mowed crabgrass. P.E. was not my forte in high school, and the goals on either side of the field left me with a sense of foreboding and sharp memories of humiliation.

4: Homopathology

Back in the auditorium, they turned off the lights, and the title of an old black and white film flickered on the screen: A Shadow in the Land. The lower part of a man's face appeared, his eyes lost in the darkness. "I know now that inside I am sick," he said, "not just sexually—I'm sick in a lot of ways. I'm immature, childlike—the sex is just a part of it—like a stomach ache is a symptom of who knows what." This was followed by dark, smoky scenes from gay bars in the early 'sixties. A voice-over helped us make sense of what we were seeing. "Homosexuality is a diseased, pathological condition. Commasculation, or homosexuality between men, is in fact a mental illness which has reached epidemiological proportions."

The next scene showed two men sitting at a table with their hands on each other's thighs, a couple slow-dancing in the haze, two men kissing in the shadows. "The 'Happy Homosexual' is a contradiction in terms," the voice continued. "The so-called 'gay lifestyle' belies the actual homosexual condition. A true, obligatory homosexual automatically rules out the possibility that he will remain happy for long."

The camera zoomed in on a forlorn man sitting at a table, his tie undone, lipstick smeared across his lips, clasping a bottle of whiskey. The shadow of another man fell across the table. "The homosexual is never normal, never happy, never satisfied. He is condemned to leading a desperately lonely and isolated life." We heard a door slam—then the man knocked the bottle over and sobbed into his arms. I cringed at the abject hopelessness of this sordid world.

Next, another title flickered on the screen: The Twilight World of Butches. This film, also in black and white, showed husky women dressed like men in coats and ties dancing with women wearing party dresses. Another ominous, disembodied voice explained the scene: "Notorious for preying on innocent wallflowers, these unscrupulous butches enslave unfortunate girls who have been rejected by men." The film showed the bulldykes smoking cigars as they hitched up their trousers and leered at the femmes, who flirted coquettishly. "These she-devils bend and twist the wills of these poor girls in a post-hypnotic trance to do their bidding."

The fluorescent lights came up, and Ruth came out on the stage and stood at the podium. We all squinted and blinked till our pupils adjusted to the brightness. Ruth's manner was serious, even stern, punctuating her speech with significant pauses and vigorous thrusts of her pointer.

"Despite the crude attempts by the homosexual lobby to whitewash their disorder," she began, "we now have a thorough understanding of the homosexual affliction. Homopathology is a mental and spiritual disorder caused by a disturbance in the dysfunctional family configuration. Everyone is innately heterosexual. The only time you have a homosexual outcome is when your intrinsic heterosexuality, your altrigenderism, has been blocked by wretched childhood experiences. Reparative therapy represents the final solution to this stubborn, persistent, and pernicious problem."

The lights dimmed again, and a slide came up on the screen: "From Sexual Brokenness to Sexual Maturity—Steps Out of Homosexuality." Ruth touched the screen with her pointer as she read the next slide: "'Homosexuality is the outward reflection of sexual brokenness.'" We all copied this down in our notebooks. "'Heterosexuality,' on the other hand, 'is the outward reflection of inner wholeness.'" She paused for a moment to let this sink in.

"Research has shown that homosexuality in the male is caused by a close-binding, intrusive mother, and a distant father. Nevertheless, where a boy has a warm and manly relationship with his father, he never becomes homosexual, irregardless of what the mother was like. In the female, homosexuality is caused by incest or other childhood sexual abuse."

In my own case, of course, my father had split altogether. And although we fought all the time, I guess you could say my mother was binding and intrusive. I sank in my seat to hear how closely I fit the profile.

"Think about what this means: the young boy is looking for his lost father in a desperate desire to break away from the hyper-feminization of the mother. The young girl is seeking refuge from her exploitation, a safe harbor at the breast of another woman. It's not their fault; no one should blame the young person for distorted sexual leanings. It's only the acting out of these debased tendencies that inevitably leads to sin.

"This disturbance results in an insecure sense of masculinity or femininity. You seek out a homosexual relationship in a misguided attempt to resolve this confusion about whether you're a man or a woman. But this quest is doomed to failure," she said, ominously.

"The boy thinks he can attract another man by becoming like his mother. He is drawn to manly men, since this is the quality he is missing, but of course masculine men are repulsed by effeminacy."

Jackson leaned over to me. "You'd be amazed," he whispered, "how many 'manly men' like chicks with dicks." I blinked in surprise at this confession.

"Besides," Ruth continued, "a real man would never be attracted to another male, irregardless of his masculinity. The pitiful homosexual is destined to furtive encounters in public toilets and other sordid rendezvous with older deviants who are even more desperate than he is. What a lost and troubled soul!"

I thought about my experiences under the piers and railroad trestles, getting a wank in dirty bookstores, and shuddered.

"The girl, on the other hand, hates men—for understandable reasons, since she has been so exploited by them—yet paradoxically, she becomes like a man in order to attract a woman. But no real woman is attracted to a tomboy—" here she glared at Sheila, who tilted her chin and looked away—"so she is destined to be used by some diesel dyke or bull dagger who is even more masculine than she is, thus perpetuating her previous abuse."

Sheila squirmed, do doubt in response to her own unfortunate history.

Ruth seemed to be on the upswing. "As a boy, you felt that something was missing. You have the mistaken notion that you want to possess another man, when what you really want is to be a man!"

Jackson held up his hand and asked, "What about those studies that say homosexuality can be inherited?"

Ruth's nostrils flared with a quick intake of breath. "Homosexuals are not born, they are made! Given the right circumstances—or I should say the wrong circumstances—anyone could become homosexual. Anyone!" She whacked the podium with her pointer. "Our prisons are full of homosexuals. Look at boarding schools, monasteries, and the Priesthood! Even the military—the Army, the Navy, the Air Force, dare I say even the Marine Corps—every one of the armed forces we depend upon to protect us from foreign invasion is rife, yes, rife with the internal rot of circumstantial homosexuality!" She narrowed her eyes and glared at us. "Once you let someone of the same sex kiss you, you'll never want anything else!"

I bounced against the back of my seat. So that's how it was! In the Boy Scouts, I yearned for Matt to kiss me when he wrapped his arms around me, tying the bowline. I thanked my lucky stars it never came to that, as much as I longed for it.

Ruth continued: "Even if there were some truth to the theory of genetic predisposition—which I sincerely doubt, since these are flawed studies, concocted by avowed homosexuals—shall we give up on the sick homosexual any more than we give up on the diseased alcoholic? I say, No way! No way on God's green earth will I ever let this homosexual conspiracy go unchallenged!" The color rose on her neck, and she poured herself a glass of water at the podium.

"So," she continued, "as I was saying, before we got slightly derailed," here she gave a little laugh, "we have an insecure sense of masculinity in the homosexual male, and an insecure sense of femininity in the female.

"Our program is designed to correct this imbalance by providing a restoration of one's natural gender role. To that end, the young men will be immersed in a regimen of sports and rigorous athletic challenges, which will mobilize the masculine energy and increase the testosterone to normal levels. Vigorous sports, manly friendship, and intensive sexual realignment therapy with someone of the same gender can help you build a more secure masculine identity. We will unblock your heterosexuality by repairing your childhood through a healing relationship with a virile father figure, the good father that you never had: the Reverend Slocock.

"Similarly, we provide makeover classes for the ladies: some of our girls have never had a perm or had their nails done. Many have never even worn make-up! Once made over by our volunteer beauticians, you'd be surprised how many of our girls are really knock-outs. You'll be so pleased to discover there's no need for despair, you really can be attractive to a man, after all." (Sheila flinched.)

"If your determination to change is strong enough, if you have the right amount of true motivation and genuine support, you can be delivered from the homosexual lifestyle and become reborn in the fellowship of Jesus. The rest is up to you. Where there's a will, there's only one way—for Jesus!"

By the end of her lecture, my confidence was shaken. I could tell from her piercing glare that everything she said was directed at me. My father abandoned me; I fell in love with my best friends, who were never available; I had sordid sex with strangers; and I was terrible at sports. She had obviously seen right through me. I was certain I could never live up to the rigorous routine she had laid out for us.

5: Pride Goeth before the Fall

When I came to Sly's office for my initial therapy, I was ready to call it quits. I so closely fit the profile that Ruth had revealed to us, I wasn't sure anymore there was any point in even trying to change.

Reverend Slocock wore his usual camouflaged fatigues, no doubt expecting an air raid at any moment. He sat with his boots on his desk, his hands clasped behind his head. His belt buckle sported the "Don't Tread On Me" flag from the Revolutionary War. Beneath the snake, in embossed letters, was the challenge, "Try and burn this one." He wore a blue baseball cap with the slogan, "POW-MIAs: You are not forgotten."

"Sit down, son." He motioned to a chair which had a leather flight jacket draped over the back. It sported a map of Vietnam with "VF-117 Privateers" embroidered across the top. "That's my squadron. On the right shoulder you'll see a patch from the Special Forces at An Khe that rescued me after my chopper was shot down." I found the skull and cross bones insignia. The skull wore a red beret.

I looked around his office. A model of PT 109 sat on his desk, its tiny torpedoes lined up, ready for fire. A gunrack held an assortment of rifles above a faded "Dream Girl, '68" poster. A buxom blond girl wearing boots and a star-spangled bikini waved two six-shooters, with palm trees swaying in the background. "That's from the old Caravelle Social Club, in Saigon. Oh the times we had," he said, and winked.

I dreaded the possibility he would go into more detail, but since I didn't pick up on it, he let it drop.

27

"Can I interest you in a cigar?" Sly held out a felt-lined box. I declined. "Just as well, they're no good for you. Another bad habit I picked up in Nam." He held one up to his nose. "These are nine-inch Hemingways, with a cameroon wrapper and a ring size of 52." He bit off the end and spat it into the trash can. "You know what that means?"

I shook my head.

"That means it's a big fat stogie." He laughed. "Not that I'm a size queen." He glanced at me to gauge my reaction as he lit his cigar. He cheeks swelled like bellows, then he blew out the match. "You know what agastopia is?" I shook my head. "That's the admiration for a certain body part." I must have looked a bit shocked. "A homosexual joke, son, relax. Just testing to see how far you've been acculturated into the lifestyle." He held the cigar between his thumb and first two fingers, and looked at it admiringly. "'Sometimes a cigar is just a cigar.' Freud said that." Then he turned again toward me, and blew a puff of smoke. "I can tell by looking at you, you're a homo-phony."

"A what?" I asked and then coughed, a little nervous.

"It's a musical term: usually pronounced ho-MA-fo-nee. It means 'in a single voice.' A single, pure and innocent voice."

"I don't quite follow."

"You may be tempted to stray from the true path, but your heart is not corrupted. I am a student of physiognomy, the analysis of character revealed through facial features, and you are what I would call a pseudo-homosexual."

"You think I'm not really gay?"

"You are not what's commonly known as 'an obligatory homosexual.' It's obvious that homosexuality is not what you really want, which makes the Lord's task that much easier. Not that you weren't in the gravest danger when I plucked you out of the gutter." He leaned back and blew a smoke ring. "But you are ripe for salvation, which is more than I can say about some of your feasless classmates.

"This batch is full of unk-unks," Sly continued. "Unknown quantities. Despite being a pious Bibleback, Perry's a confirmed catamite. Jackson's nothing but a boony rat, an unpredictable abbeylubber. And that Sheila is boo coo dyke. They all suffer from abulia, a total lack of spine, of willpower. They're going to be tough nuts to crack."

I felt embarrassed by his characterizations of my fellow inductees, though I had similar first impressions.

"With you, however, I am a confirmed antinomian," he said.

"Excuse me?"

"Faith will see you through. Through and through, my friend, through and through."

I nodded, although after Ruth's lecture, I was no where near as optimistic. I felt uncertain about his faith in me, since I had so little faith in my own ability to change. I looked away, afraid he would sense my doubts, and found myself staring at a letter he had framed on the wall.

"Oh, that," he said. He swung his feet off the desk, and leaned forward. "I accused "Sesame Street" of promoting homosexuality with those two queers they got on the show, what are their names, yeah, Bert and Ernie. They live together, go everywhere together, my God! They even sleep in the same room. They are for all intents and purposes a married couple. "Sesame Street" had the gall to write back to me and say 'Bert and Ernie are not gay, they are puppets.' Yeah, they're puppets all right, puppets of the Devil! Just like those sissy little lavender Teletubbies, cooing and mewing, turning all our kids into a bunch of pansies. And Barney! That big blimp brontosaurus. A New Age Anti-Christ, is what he is. Patooee, is what I say. Of course, before I found the Lord, I used to say a lot worse." He chuckled.

"Then there's Frog and Toad, those amphibious frauds, corrupting children's literature." Sly reached into his drawer and pulled out a copy of *Frog and Toad Are Friends*. "Let me tell you, Frog and Toad are more than just friends. That's code for 'very special friends.' Why they might as well be lovers!" He flipped through the pages while puffs of smoke chugged out of his cigar. "Where are their mothers, sisters, and girlfriends? Where are all the little tadpoles?" He pointed out various pages with shocked disgust. "Look at this! Toad brings Frog some tea in bed; Frog jumps naked into the pond; Frog and Toad sitting together with their arms around each other. Best friends, bah! This is a thinly disguised homo-amphibious world, utterly devoid of the soft humanizing touch of a feminine frog."

I reached for the book, but Sly shoved it into the drawer and slammed it shut.

"Of course there is a time and place for the menfolk to get together in the army, relax in our clubs, slap some butt in the locker room to build espirit de corps. But this masculine camaraderie has to be balanced by communion with the fair sex, lest one become unbalanced and begin to crave the unnatural satisfaction of carnal desire and bestial lust!"

He stood up and took another puff on his cigar. "This is the basic law of antisyzygy—the union of opposites. Man was made in God's image with the capacity for higher enjoyments—" here he pointed his cigar at me—"yet there's a bit of the devil in him, too." He strutted behind his desk, his head erect, waving his cigar in broad gestures. "A woman tames and soothes the wild beast and civilizes his base nature, offers respite from his torment." Then he turned and stared at me, narrowing his eyes. "Yet she can also turn into a dangerous temptress! The Devil is lurking everywhere." He pounded the desk. "Everywhere! Only in the matrimonial bed can man's true nature express itself without corrupting the spirit."

I was feeling a bit dizzy from all the cigar smoke, combined with his odd oration. Yet I was intrigued by the slender thread of hope he dangled for my personal salvation. I waved my hand to clear the air.

"Oh, here, let's turn on the fan. I didn't mean to asphyxiate you."

From the ceiling fan hung a model of an airplane with two propellers on each wing, a big R in a circle on its tail. It began to rotate beneath the fan. Sly pointed to it with his cigar. "Enola Gay, the bomber that dropped the Big One on Japan." He reflected on that momentous event. "That's what I hate about the homosexuals ruining a perfectly good word like 'gay!' Gay used to mean happy or carefree! You're too young to even remember that."

"I guess so," I said, and looked at his bookcase, which held titles like *Unhappy Gays, Straight is the Way, The Homosexual Deception, None Dare Call It Perversion,* and *An Urgent Message of Warning to Gay Men.*

Sly sat down again at his desk. "My God, you can't even call them queer anymore, since they've taken to calling themselves homos and fruits and fairies as if they were genuinely proud of it, which I don't believe for one second. Not for a single solitary second!" He punctuated each word by jutting the air with his cigar. "I can spot a reaction formation when I see it. You know what a reaction formation is?"

I could guess, but I shook my head, since he so obviously wanted to tell me.

"A reaction formation is when you want to do one thing, but you do the opposite because you can't stand to think of yourself that way. Gay pride is a prime example. They feel loathsome for what they do, as well they should, since lying with another man is an abomination before the Lord, but do they cringe in terror? No! They have the gall to say they are proud of it. Proud of it! Ha! Pride goeth before the Fall! You know and I know they are not fooling you, and they're sure as hell not fooling me. So who do you think they're fooling?"

I knew this was the punch line, so I held my tongue.

"Themselves, that's who!" The Rev leaned back again in his chair and clasped his hands behind his head, basking in his psychological and spiritual triumph.

Though obviously a blowhard, his words still worked their spell on me. I hoped for my own sake Sly was right—I was a homo-phony, and would soon be made whole.

6: Abominations

After lunch, we were supposed to meet with Ruth in the Fireside Room, a far more inviting space than the auditorium. It had a stone fireplace, a piano, and a circle of comfy chairs. Before she arrived, I looked over the large bookcase, which held a stack of hymnals, and some more books with titles similar to ones I'd seen at Sly's: *You Don't Have to Be Gay*, *Steps Out of Homosexuality*, *The Hidden Homosexual Agenda*, *Making Sin a Civil Right*, and *Gay Lib or Gay Fib?*

I looked around the room. Sheila had flung one leg over the arm of her chair and filed her nails with intense concentration. Perry was sitting with his head bowed, intently studying a Bible he held open on his lap. Jackson came in and sat next to Sheila. "Aren't we demure today?" Sheila ignored him. He tried to pull her shoelace, but she jerked her foot away.

Ruth entered the room carrying a stack of Bibles. "Welcome to Bible Study," she said. "These are your own personal Bibles, which you may keep. Feel free to mark inspiring passages." She passed them out, along with some pencils.

"The Revised Standard Version," Perry said with an exasperated air. "If you don't mind, I prefer to keep my King James."

"It's the standard Protestant version, without all the thees and thous," Ruth explained. "We've sent away for the Scofield Reference Bible, but in the meantime, this will have to do. It's easier to understand, and we can all follow along on the same page."

"I like the 'thees' and 'thous,'" Perry mumbled. But he put down his own Bible and started thumbing through one of the RSVs.

Ruth said, "This is the time set aside for us to pursue a serious exegesis of God's Word. Do you know what 'exegesis' means?"

"It means you're no longer a Christian?" Jackson volunteered.

"Absolutely not," Ruth said, flustered. "Wherever did you get such a notion?"

"Ex-Jesus, isn't that what you said?"

"Heavens, no," Ruth said, stifling a laugh. "It's exegesis, not ex-Jesus. It means a close and careful reading of the Scriptures, so we can understand the Word of God."

"Sounds like 'ex-Jesus' to me," Jackson said.

Ruth pursed her lips, but went on. "Homosexuality is against Scripture. Let's turn to Deuteronomy 22:5." We all opened our Bibles, most of us fumbling for some time before locating the table of contents.

Perry said, "It's on page 153."

"Thank you, Perry. Has everyone found it? Why don't you read it for us, Perry."

"'A woman shall not wear anything that pertains to a man, nor shall a man put on a woman's garment; for whoever does these things is an abomination to the Lord your God.'"

Ruth said, "Thank you, Perry. This is pretty clear, now, isn't it?"

Jackson narrowed his eyes. It was obvious Ruth had chosen just this passage to skewer his own predilections.

Sheila said, "Who's to say what's men's clothing and what's women's clothing? Look at the Pope, running around in that ridiculous dress and caftan."

"Of course fashions change with the times," Ruth said. "What's important here is that God doesn't want to catch you cross-dressing."

"You can't fool God," Jackson said.

"No, you can't fool God," Ruth agreed. "But there is the danger that you might mislead someone of the same gender."

"Quelle horrible," Jackson said.

"Now let's continue. In Genesis, 19:5, when Lot welcomed two angels to his home, the men of Sodom surrounded his house: 'and they called out to Lot, "Where are the men who came to you tonight? Bring them out to us, that we may know them."' This was an abomination in the eyes of the Lord. After Lot and his family escaped, God punished the men of Sodom: 'Then the Lord rained on Sodom and Gomorrah brimstone and fire.'"

Sheila said, "I don't see why He had to turn Lot's wife into a pillar of salt. All she did was look back."

"God told her not to," Perry said.

"She was only curious," Sheila insisted. "And God had just promised Abraham He wouldn't destroy the town if there were at least ten innocent people in Sodom. What about all the women and children God killed with the fire and brimstone?"

"He probably just killed the men," Perry said.

"How could that be?" Sheila demanded. "He wiped out the whole town!"

"He's God!" Perry countered. "He can do anything he wants!"

Ruth said, "Please, let's get back to our focus for today, shall we?"

Sheila said, "Wait! We skipped right over the part where Lot offers his daughters in place of the angels. 'Behold, I have two daughters who have not known man; let me bring them out to you, and do to them as you please.' Didn't God think that was a little tacky?"

Ruth seemed to be taken aback. "Well it's far better to marry off your daughters than to allow your sons to be sodomized."

"But I thought they wanted to rape them!" Sheila said.

Perry had flipped ahead. "Deuteronomy 22:28 says if you rape a woman, you have to pay off the father and marry her."

Sheila sat up in her chair, and looked for Deuteronomy. "What? If you rape a woman she has to marry you? That is so gross!"

Perry said, "Well in those days, no man would ever marry a woman who wasn't a virgin. At least this law forced them to take responsibility for the goods they had spoiled."

"That's exactly what I'm talking about!" Sheila said. "Women are treated like chattel, or spoiled goods!"

Ruth interrupted this exchange and said, "I think we are straying far afield from our current task. God condemns any violation of His natural law. Now let's look at Leviticus 18:22. 'Thou shalt not lie with a man as with a woman—It is an abomination!'"

"Ooh, yuck," Sheila squealed. "Deuteronomy 25:11 says a woman who seizes the private parts of a man who is beating her husband should have her hand cut off!"

Perry said, "That's because a man whose balls have been crushed can't go to heaven. Look at Deuteronomy 23:1."

"Oh!" cried Jackson, who clutched himself protectively at the very thought.

"Or if you cut off his dick," Perry added.

"Perry," Ruth said sternly, "I will thank you not to use such vulgar language, especially in the presence of ladies."

"Well his 'male member,' then. It's in the Bible."

Sheila jumped in again. "But why should a woman who's protecting her husband, or a man who's been castrated, be treated so cruelly? It's not their fault!" she cried.

"The Lord works in mysterious ways," said Perry.

"I think we keep getting distracted from the main point," Ruth said. "There are a few more Biblical prohibitions against homosexuality we need to cover. Let's look at Romans 1:26-27: 'For this reason God gave them up to dishonorable passions. Their women exchanged natural relations for unnatural, and the men likewise gave up natural relations with women and were consumed with passion for one another—"

Jackson said, "Who's to say what's 'natural'?"

"God," said Perry.

"Then why did God give them up?" asked Sheila.

Ruth ignored this question and continued: "'men committing shameless acts with men and receiving in their own persons the due penalty for their error.' What do you suppose that means?"

Perry said, "AIDS, of course."

Ruth nodded, gravely. "AIDS is a plague of the end times. AIDS is a consequence of the Fall—as all disease is—and separation from God. Mankind has bought into Satan's lie that freedom comes from throwing off the restraints of God. But that kind of freedom actually enslaves people. Sheila, would you like to read First Corinthians 6:9-10?"

"'Do not be deceived; neither the immoral, nor idolaters, nor adulterers, nor homosexuals, nor thieves, nor the greedy, nor drunkards, nor revilers, nor robbers will inherit the kingdom of God.'"

Perry said, "That's what I don't like about the RSV. The word 'homosexual' wasn't even invented until a hundred years ago. Malakoi means effeminate, and Arsenokoitai probably referred to street hustlers."

Jackson winced. Ruth said, "The point is, with promiscuous behavior, adultery, or fornication, you'll go straight to hell. Galatians 5:19-21, 'Now the works of the flesh are plain: immorality, impurity, licentiousness, idolatry, sorcery, enmity, strife, jealousy, anger, selfishness, dissension, party spirit—'"

"Whoa!" Jackson exclaimed. "No more partying?"

Ruth furrowed her brow and continued: "envy, drunkenness, carousing, and the like. I warn you, as I warned you before, that those who do such things shall not inherit the kingdom of God.'"

"Quelle bummer," Jackson said.

"This is serious business," Ruth said. "As you can see in Leviticus 20:13, your very salvation is in question. 'If a man lies with a male as with a woman, both of them have committed an abomination; they shall be put to death, their blood is upon them.'"

"Oh, jeez," Jackson said. "They ain't none of us goin' to heaven, if that's the case."

"You can repent," Perry said, hopefully.

Meanwhile, Sheila had been flipping feverishly back and forth between chapters. "Here are all these laws in Leviticus saying who not to sleep with: you can't sleep with your neighbor's wife, or your wife's mother, or your daughter-in-law, or with a beast, or your sister, or your aunt or your uncle's wife, or your brother's wife—unless your brother has died, and then you have to marry her, whether she wants to or not—but there's nothing here about sleeping with your own daughter. Then in Genesis 19, Lot's daughters sleep with him and have his children. Does the Bible condone incest?"

Ruth shook her head, obviously agitated. "These were special circumstances, of course. Since all the men in Sodom and Gomorrah had been killed, Lot's daughters had no men available to them to sire their children. And Lot was asleep, so he had no carnal pleasure."

"Just a wet dream," Jackson sniggered.

"So are you saying what's right depends on the circumstances?" asked Sheila.

"'What's right,'" said Perry, "is whatever God says is right."

"You can't take these incidents out of their historical context," Ruth reminded us.

It all started sounding like moral relativism to me.

Jackson fidgeted in his chair. "So it all depends on our own interpretation, or what?"

"I'm glad you asked," Ruth said. "Listen to Second Peter 1:20: 'First of all you must understand this, that no prophecy of scripture is a matter of one's own interpretation.' That's because 'no prophecy ever came by the impulse of man, but men moved by the Holy Spirit spoke from God.'"

"But how do we know it was inspired by God?" Sheila asked. "Couldn't anyone claim God spoke to him?"

"'Cause it's in the Bible," Perry said.

Ruth nodded. "Remember in Genesis 3, the Serpent cast doubt upon God's command by asking Eve, 'Did God say, "You shall not eat of any tree of the Garden?"' This conniving question led directly to the Fall. And who do you suppose was responsible for planting the seed of doubt in Eve's mind?"

Jackson opened his eyes wide and rubbed his chin in a thoughtful way. "Could it be…Satan?"

Sheila laughed.

Ruth said, "That's not funny, young lady. Jackson is exactly right. What God had made perfectly clear, Satan was trying to confuse for his own evil plan. In the words of 1 Timothy 4:1, 'Now the Spirit expressly says that in later times some will depart from the Faith by giving heed to deceitful spirits and doctrines of demons.'"

"Demons?" I asked.

Ruth peered at me over her glasses. "Beware of cultists and tricksters," she said. "Second Timothy 3:4 warns us that in the last days, men will become 'lovers of pleasure rather than lovers of God.' What God said is plain, self-evident, and unequivocal. It's not for you to question His Word."

Ruth shut the Good Book. "For our next lesson, please read the second chapter of Second Peter and advise yourselves of the consequences of spreading false prophecies. I think that's enough for one day. I hope you will all bring a less contentious attitude, and a more open heart to God's Word tomorrow."

* * *

Later, lying on my bunk, I read this section from Second Peter: "But false prophets also arose among the people, just as there will be false teachers among you, who will secretly bring in destructive heresies…bringing upon themselves swift destruction. And many will follow their licentiousness, and because of them the way of truth will be reviled. And in their greed they will exploit you with false words….

"For if God did not spare the angels when they sinned, but cast them into hell and committed them to pits of nether gloom to be kept until the

Judgment; if He did not spare the ancient world…when He brought a flood upon the world of the ungodly; if by turning the cities of Sodom and Gomorrah to ashes He condemned them to extinction…then the Lord knows how to rescue the godly from trial, and to keep the unrighteous under punishment until the day of judgment, especially those who indulge in the lust of defiling passion."

The notion of going to hell for my homosexuality was new to me. Of course I'd heard it condemned before, but I never realized God took it so personally. Now hellfire and brimstone rose before me with a fearsome roar. Yet, being at risk for making the worst mistake in my life strangely appealed to me. Even eternal damnation held an exotic allure—not that I wanted to go to hell, but to sense its presence as an imminent danger thrilled me—like skating on thin ice, scrambling up a dangerous cliff, or sky-diving.

I was uncertain that I was up to such a challenge, yet the possibility of abysmal failure sent shivers up my spine that were strangely pleasurable. I could almost understand how some Christians fall back into homosexuality, or even have unsafe sex. It's probably the best chance we have of tempting hell on earth.

7: Petticoats and Pigskin

"I am a firm believer in muscular Christianity," Sly announced. He stood in front of us on the playing field wearing a tank-top and gym shorts. He wasn't in bad shape for his fifties. Jackson, Perry, and I clutched our chests and hopped around on the wet grass to keep warm while the fog billowed around us.

"Jesus was a carpenter, not a wimp! He had well-developed muscles and strong, sinewy arms." Sly held up one arm and tightened his biceps. "He was a masculine, upstanding specimen of a man, who stood tall, defiant, and erect!" Sly stood at attention and saluted. "Remember! Armageddon will be fought on the field as well as in heaven."

Then he outlined this elaborate conspiracy theory that troops from the United Nations are hiding in secret bunkers in salt mines beneath Detroit. At a pre-arranged signal from the international banking cartel, they will emerge in black helicopters and take over the country using shock troops provided by inner city gangs and groups like Homo Nation to disarm the unsuspecting populace and create a One-World dictatorship, led by the Anti-Christ, that would reign for a thousand years.

"Gangstas and queer boys?" Jackson said, doubtfully. "I don't think so."

Sly dismissed his skepticism with contempt. "You have no idea what we're up against." He then filled us in on numerous UFO sightings, hushed up by the government, that foreshadow the imminent arrival of the Seven Angels and Seven Plagues prophesied in Revelations. "But enough of theory," Sly said. "It's time to practice and prepare for the Apocalypse."

He blew his whistle and led us through some warm-ups—jumping jacks, toe-touches, and push-ups. "Keep your backs straight! I don't want to see your butts bobbing in the air!"

Then he had us do wind-sprints from one goal to the other. After ten lengths my eyes watered and I gasped for breath, my lungs seared by the cold wind. Perry, his cheeks flushed, collapsed on the ground. Jackson rested his hands on his knees, gulping in air.

Sly blew his whistle. "Come on, men! Let's show Jesus you're not a bunch of pansies! Perry! Up and at 'em!" Perry pulled himself off the ground, and we fell back in line.

"Football mobilizes the masculine energy and increases your testosterone," he said as he shoved strips of cloth into our shorts to play flag football. "No more niminy-piminy."

It was Sly and Perry against me and Jackson. Perry bent over and Sly stuck his hands between his legs. "Hup one, hup two, hut!" Sly backed up while Perry raced ahead for the pass. Jackson and I rushed toward Sly, who side-stepped us and passed to Perry, who, of course, fumbled it.

He and Perry huddled for their next move. I looked at Jackson. "What surprise maneuver do you think they'll pull this time?"

Jackson shrugged. "A naked reverse, or a Hail Mary?"

This time, Perry played quarterback. "Eighty-six, ninety-three, fourteen—" Sly hiked the ball, then held his elbows out to the sides and rammed right into Jackson and me, knocking us both on our butts. Meanwhile, the ball sailed over Perry's head. He ran after it, then streaked past us for the goal.

"Get up, you lubbers!" Sly roared. "After him!" Jackson scrambled to his feet, and I chased Perry toward the endzone.

When he made the touchdown, Sly was in heaven. "Yahoo!" He grabbed Perry, rubbed his knuckles in his hair, and growled with delight. "Thataboy! What a tiger!" Sly took the ball from him and shoved it back in his stomach. "You see, you can do it!"

"Oomph!" Perry said, and looked down at the ball. "Oh my God!" he exclaimed, and dropped it.

"What? What's the matter?" asked Sly.

"Is that really a—pigskin?"

"Genuine article!"

Perry had a look of horror upon his face. "That's, that's…an abomination!"

"What the hell are you talking about?" Sly demanded.

"He's gone loony tunes," Jackson said, lifting the ball.

"Don't touch it!" Perry cried. "The swine is unclean!"

Jackson dropped it. "What is it? Dog doo?"

"Of all the nuttiness I have ever heard," Sly said. "Football is an A-1 all-American sport!" He lifted the football and held it lace-side up. "Look, it's signed by O.J. Simpson."

Perry raised his eyes toward heaven. "'Of their flesh thou shalt not eat, and their carcasses thou shalt not touch; they are unclean!' Leviticus 11:8." He fell on his knees and clasped his hands together, praying to God for forgiveness.

Sly stood there with his hands on his hips. "Well what do you expect us to play with? Plastic?"

Perry refused to play again until Jackson found a nerfball in the playbox back in the Fireside Room—a pink football about the size of a grapefruit, which squeaked when you squeezed it and made a whiffling sound when you tossed it through the air. Jackson giggled. By this time, Sly had lost much of his enthusiasm.

After a few more skirmishes, Sly bundled us into the bunkhouse and insisted we take cold showers. "It hardens the constitution," he claimed. He stood in the doorway to the bathroom while we stripped and turned on the jetspray. He watched us, he said, just to make sure we didn't cheat. All three of us dashed in and out of the spray so fast we barely got damp.

Then Sly took off his clothes and stood under the spray, shaking his head and blowing water through his lips. "Ahhh-yah!" he shouted, then shut off the shower. "Rejuvenation and cleansing with primal waters," he proclaimed. He toweled himself off with a vigorous sawing motion across his back, his manhood swaying like a massive pendulum. I looked away.

While I was drying my hair, he reached out and squeezed the biceps of my left arm. "You boys are coming along fine," he said, and winked.

After getting dressed, we headed back toward the Fireside Room and spied this lady holding a high-heel shoe in one hand as she hobbled across the grass. She was decked out in a ruffled dress, with a bouffant hair-do and bangle bracelets. "Is that a new recruit?" asked Perry.

"My God! It's Sheila!" Jackson squealed. He ran up to her and kissed her on the cheek.

"This," she said, holding her arms out to the side, "is the Outward Reflection of my Inner Wholeness."

"You're gorgeous!" Jackson said.

"She looks like a drag queen," Perry said.

Sheila nodded, and burst into tears. "I have never been so humiliated in all my life. Look at me!" She displayed her gaudily-painted nails. "Fuchsia!" she exclaimed. She held up her broken heel. "Stilettos!" She shook her head, but her hair swayed back and forth in one block, like a helmet. "Hairspray!" She raised her dress over her ankle. "Nylons!"

"You got a run, dear," Jackson said, consolingly.

She pointed to her cheeks, her lips, her eyes: "Rouge! Lipstick! Eye shadow!" she cried. "Eye liner! Mascara!" Which was now running in a black rivulet down her cheek, carving a path through her foundation of pancake.

Jackson hugged her and she sobbed on his shoulder. After she recovered herself, she told us what happened.

"Ruth decided a ladylike makeover would help me reclaim my innate femininity. She recruited a volunteer from Francine's Beauty College, this dame who looked like she'd just stepped out of a Doris Day movie. 'We're ladies helping lesbians become ladies,' she explained. 'We'll fuss over you, pamper you, and show you how pretty you can be. We'll help you develop a feminine image of yourself you never suspected was even possible!'"

"You got that right!" Jackson said.

"Then she said, 'Once you see how beautiful you really are, you'll begin to believe in your inner femininity. Many of the girls we've seen never felt confident enough to break away from their butch demeanor—the kind of look that makes a man run the other way. This masculine masquerade needs to be completely broken down, and then built up again with a new feminine foundation!'

"Then she spun me around to face the mirror. 'Take a good look at yourself, honey. Your new appearance reflects your wholeness, not your brokenness.'

"Now look at me! I can't even walk straight!" She leaned on Jackson's shoulder and took off her other shoe.

"We just come back from football," Jackson said, in a gruff voice. "Till the man, here, decided the pigskin was unclean."

"What?" Sheila looked at Perry.

"It's in Leviticus," said Perry, "along with all the other abominations. You're not supposed to even touch it."

"So we had to play with this nerfball," I added, holding up the pink football. "I think Sly was disappointed."

Sheila laughed, and grabbed the ball. She tossed it to me, I threw it to Jackson, then we played pickle with her in the middle. She slid into Jackson and tore her stockings and ruined her coif.

Back at the house, Ruth gave her a sour expression. "I'm trying!" Sheila protested, holding the shoe with the broken heel. She looked sheepishly at the grass stains on her new party dress. Her nylons were shredded.

Ruth shook her head as she spread glue on the heel. "How you expect to find a husband when you carry on like a wild tomboy, I'll never know."

Looking at Sheila, I wondered whether certain tendencies weren't simply a part of our natural temperament.

Ruth smiled, half to herself, as she screwed the vice holding the shoe. "Even the Lord needs a little assistance in working a miracle."

8: Exorcism

Our HomoAnon meeting was open once a week to Escape graduates and others who couldn't take the time to do a live-in program, but who wanted to keep in touch with the group. We brought some folding chairs into the Fireside Room, and about ten people showed up. Ruth led the meeting. We started out with the Lord's Prayer, then went through the Fourteen Steps and admitted we were powerless over homosexuality, rather than alcohol (although some confessed they were powerless over both). I guess we needed fourteen steps instead of the usual twelve because homosexuality is a more fully entrenched disease than alcoholism.

Ruth explained that as a special treat for the newcomers (that's us), tonight's focus would be on testimonials of the healing power of Escape.

"Hello, my name is Sally." Sally was a plump woman in a polka dot dress, who kept her knees together and held a small white Bible with gilded pages in her lap. "It is virtually impossible to be happy in the homosexual lifestyle."

An older man with a walrus moustache named Irwin spoke next. "The struggle with same-sex attraction is like a parasite that sucks the very life out of you."

"Following the program is like being in a pressure cooker," Sally added. "All the sin rises to the surface, all our hurts and wounds and same-sex desire."

Steve, a portly man in a striped suit, said, "I realized that if I truly wanted to walk with Jesus I had to leave my lover. I loved him with all my heart, but felt that I had to serve Christ. I only wanted what the Bible tells us is best for us." His eyes were moist. When he finished talking, so were mine.

"My therapist told me if I let a woman kiss me I would be ruined for life," said Sandra, who had a deep crease between her eyes. "When my girlfriend finally kissed me, we both realized we were taking on this curse. So I broke it off."

They continued with a rapid-fire barrage of testimonials, one after another, each more alarming than the rest:

"Homosex is against God's will."

"There's a void at the heart of homosexuality."

"It's crooked at its basic root."

"It's a false self."

"It's ill-adapted, outrageous, and rude."

"Immoral, sinful, and self-destructive."

"Venal, vile, and vulgar."

"Inherently repulsive."

"It's a tragic lifestyle of bondage."

"You have two deviant people coming together, and what can you expect?"

Steve said, "I'm a recent graduate, and I'm living a life that I would consider obedient under the standards that God has given me. That doesn't mean I never have a homosexual thought, but I just got my first anniversary chip for abstinence."

Everyone clapped. By this time I was feeling woozy. They all seemed so determined, but I felt sad about their stories. I pushed back the tears, not wanting to seem unmanly. And I wanted to be happy for them.

"Thank you, everyone!" Ruth said. "Now let's hear from the newcomers."

We looked at each other, then finally Perry got up and said, "Hi, I'm Perry."

"Hi, Perry!"

"I am very grateful to hear your inspiring stories."

Then Sheila got up. "My name is Sheila."

"Hi, Sheila!"

"I am still struggling with my sexual brokenness, but I have faith that I can be healed." Everyone clapped.

Jackson got up, and took off his cap. He quickly glanced around the circle, then down at his cap. "Hey, I'm Jackson."

"Hi, Jackson!"

"They ain't nobody never been gay in my family. So that's why I'm here."

Then it was my turn. Before the meeting, Ruth had explained that indiscretions are called "slips," while actually having sex is considered a "fall." I wasn't sure how much to confess, but I tried to take my cue from the other introductions. Ruth, who was sitting next to me, squeezed my knee and said, "Go ahead, Paul."

"Hi, my name is Paul. I am a homosexual."

"Hi, Paul!"

Ruth said, "Paul, let's say you're a recovering homosexual, or ex-gay, if you prefer.

"Should I start over?"

"Please."

"Hi, my name is Paul.

"Hi, Paul!"

"I'm an ex-gay. Or I guess I'm trying, at any rate. I'm doing the best I can. I came to believe I was powerless over my homosexuality, and a Power greater than myself was the only thing that could save me from a sad and sinful life." There, I said it!

Ruth said, "Without Jesus, you were powerless. But now you're not anymore!"

I had the distinct feeling I was doing it all wrong. After hearing the various testimonies, I wasn't sure whether controlling our sinful fantasies was the best we could hope for. "Can Jesus really heal our sexual brokenness, or will we always burn in lust for the flesh of another man?"

Ruth considered this question a blasphemous affront to the power of Jesus to heal us from any affliction. "We are powerless, but God certainly is not. Still, you have to apply yourself," she said, and patted my hand. "If you still have sinful thoughts, don't blame that on Jesus."

Ruth stood up and faced the group. "God condemns same-sex lust and Satanic worship. By the same token, every single soul who has adopted the homosexual lifestyle can give it up! God has given you Free Will to choose light over darkness, right over wrong, heterosexual love over sodomy!

"It would be so easy to give in, to throw in the towel, to cast your lot with other lost souls and rationalize your depravity by declaring 'Gay is Good.' Gay libbers suffer from anosognosia—the disbelief in one's own illness. They try to turn the tables by claiming that we good Christians have inflicted them with 'internalized homophobia.' Don't be fooled! That's the Great Deceiver whispering in your ear! These self-deluded souls refuse to recognize 'internalized homophobia' as a gift from God! It's a natural repugnancy for the unnatural. If anything, they suffer from meta-morphobia—the fear of change." The light flashed on her glasses. "Remember this, for those who cannot stick with the program, the treacle turns to brimstone!"

I wasn't sure what treacle was, but from the wildness in her eyes, she convinced me the treacle was on the very verge of brimstone, and so was I.

"When homosexuals grovel around on the floors of bars and public toilets slithering in slime, shoving lightbulbs and gerbils and God knows what up their rectums, they take on demonic powers! Here at Escape, we cleanse the soul and expel the demons from all the bodily orifices—out of the female vagina and the male organ, out of the anal canal, out of throats and mouths, if there's been an ungodly deposit of seminal fluids in any of those areas. We cleanse the body orifices with the blood of Jesus and we cast out the demonic powers of lust, lasciviousness, and every kind of filth. We provide a spiritual purgation, a roter-rooter of the soul, and exorcise the demon!"

Here she paused for a moment and scanned the room, which had become strangely quiet. "Could we have a volunteer from among the new recruits?"

We all avoided her glance, none of us very inclined to rush to the center of the circle.

"Sheila, please come on up. I sense an eagerness about you."

Sheila looked around her as though she must have been talking to someone else. "Me?"

"I don't see any other Sheila."

Sheila reluctantly rose from her seat. Ruth stood behind her and placed her hands on her shoulders.

"We need to cleanse the body and bind the demonic powers by pressing them out of the body orifices." As Ruth dug in her thumbs, Sheila started to wail.

"Hear that unearthly catterwaller? That's the demon protesting." Sheila's knees began to wobble as she sank toward the floor from the pressure of Ruth's thumbs. "Stay with us, Sheila! Breathe into it!"

Sheila started hyperventilating.

"Jesus, come into this vessel and vanquish the demon!"

I could see Sheila's hands cramping, her fingers splayed, until she finally crumpled under the pressure, and fell to her knees, sobbing.

"Yes! That's it! By George, I think we've got it! Good girl, Sheila!" Ruth patted her head like a dog. "Go on now, take a seat next to the boys."

Suddenly, Sheila's eyes rolled up. She started blinking and began to twitch, and then collapsed, thrashing about on the floor. "Oh, my God!" Steve said. "She's having a seizure!" He took his wallet and forced it between her teeth so she wouldn't bite her tongue. In a moment, it was over. She lay flat on her back, perspiring and exhausted. A couple of us knelt over her, while the rest of the group stood around in an awkward silence.

Sheila slowly raised herself. Steve and I helped her into one of the stuffed chairs. "She's all right," Steve said. "Give her some air!" The others backed away and returned to their seats.

Ruth was nonplused. "What you have just witnessed is a spiritual cleansing—but it's only the beginning of the process of reorientation which must be reinforced with rigorous discipline—a comprehensive treatment of prayer, repentance, and pastoral counseling.

"It's your choice to live a life of dignity and honor, or to grovel in the pit of passion until hell freezes over. To sit at the side of Jesus, or to burn in lust for eternity. To bask in God's love, or to follow false prophets to your everlasting doom.

"Resist! Repent, and be cured. Faith displaces doubt. Heterosexuality replaces homosexuality as light replaces darkness. Re-establish the heterosexual ethic! Rejoice in the Blood of the Lamb. I am the Light and the Way and the Life Everlasting, Amen."

*   *   *

Even though I let Jesus into my heart as best I could, there was no instant cure. I continued to be plagued by all these strange attractions to other men. I thought if I was sincerely motivated, I would be freed of all these sinful desires.

Maybe my heart was so hardened and narrow that there wasn't any room for Jesus to pry His way in. I decided I'd better bring this up with the Rev.

9: Cheesecake

For my second counseling session, we met again in Sly's office. He sat behind the desk in his chair. "How are things coming along, Paul?"

"Well, okay, I guess."

"You did yourself proud out on the field yesterday."

"Thank you, sir."

"Any doubts, hesitations, confusions I can clear up? Any spiritual dilemmas or quandaries? Questions of Scripture?"

"Well I was wondering, it seems like there's all kinds of prohibitions in Leviticus that we don't really pay much attention to anymore. Like shaving, getting tattoos, mixing two kinds of seed in one field, or wearing two kinds of cloth. Then there's the dietary laws—no shellfish or pork—"

Sly said, "That was quite a scene with Perry over the pigskin, wasn't it?"

"Yeah."

"With the New Covenant, we're no longer bound by the old dietary laws. Although I myself wear cotton—or wool, when it's cold—none of these polyester blends that are so popular nowadays. Lots more to iron, of course, but the women folk take care of that." He took a puff on his cigar. "What else can I do for you?"

"Well, how long is it supposed to take for homosexual attractions to disappear?"

"It all depends, son, on what you put into it."

"I asked Jesus to come into my heart, but I still have these strange desires. I feel so guilty."

53

"Have no doubt, if you sincerely ask Jesus into your heart, He will work His magic. It won't be easy, because once the devil has sunk in his talons, he will clasp you tenaciously! But there is no reason whatsoever to feel guilty about your feelings."

"There isn't?"

"Just remember, those dark, delicious desires are not coming from you. They're temptations from the Wicked One, that Old Serpent, the Father of Lies! You think Satan's going to let you off Scott-free? Lucifer, the Arch Fiend, needs you to carry out his awful, God-eclipsing plan. The Treacherous Tempter will never willingly let you loose! There's a battle raging right this moment within your heart, within your body, within your very soul!"

"What should I do?"

"You must fight to release yourself from the ungodly Power of Darkness! 'Get thee behind me, Satan!' That's what you have to say!"

"'Get thee behind me, Satan?'"

Sly pounded his desk. "Louder, as if you meant it!"

"Get thee behind me, Satan!"

"Great!" He punched the air. "Again! With gusto!"

"Get thee behind me, Satan!!" I shouted.

"That's the way we do it!" Sly came around his desk and slapped me on the back. Then he stood behind me and caressed my shoulders. "Of course, these are modern times, and we have other techniques at our disposal."

I shot out of the chair.

"What? What's the matter? I was just—"

I said, "No way. I saw what Ruth did to Sheila—"

"Ruth?" he said, suddenly wary. "What happened? What did she do?"

"You know, that demon possession thing. I'm sorry, but I'm just not into that."

"Oh yes, I understand. No, I was not going to push the demon out of you. I was just trying to help you relax a little bit. Tell you what. I'd like to introduce you to a little exercise."

"Haven't we exercised enough?"

Sly laughed. "Not that kind. This is sort of a calisthenics of the soul. Sit down."

I sat down, reluctantly, and he returned to his desk and re-lit his cigar. "Here at Escape, we take a multi-modal approach." He blew another one of his smoke rings. "You know what that means?"

"Uh, I don't know. Lots of different ways?"

"That's right. You're very intelligent, Paul. You catch on fast. 'The casting out of demons' is certainly an option for especially recalcitrant cases. We also have our prayer, fellowshipping, and vigorous exercise for masculine identity formation. In addition, we have developed a series of treatments to get at the psychological nexus of your distress."

"What kinds of treatments?" I asked, a little leery.

He took another puff. "Some of them are very pleasant, actually. Others are a bit more challenging. We start with the easy ones first. If the devil has only a slight hold on you, that may be sufficient. Cases like Sheila's, as you may have guessed, are a bit more troublesome. Depending on how deep the devil has sunk in his talons, we may have to dig even deeper into your psyche to root him out."

"So what did you mean by 'pleasant'?"

"Well, the first treatment is called Orgasmic Reorientation. It involves masturbation, which I'm sure you're quite accustomed to." He gave me one of his sly grins, then stuck the cigar back in his mouth.

I think I may have blushed a bit. I know it's something practically every guy does, but I don't think I'd ever admitted it to anyone.

"As you might assume, self-abuse is not something we normally endorse, but in the service of a higher good, the sin of Onan is perfectly harmless."

I gulped, my throat suddenly dry. "So what does this…exercise involve, exactly?" I just could not picture doing something like that in his office.

"Relax. This is something you can practice in the privacy of your own bunk. Here's what it involves: you simply masturbate imagining your usual homosexual fantasy until you are close to climax, and then at the point of inevitability you switch your fantasy to a girl." He reached into his drawer and pulled out a Playboy. "In case there's no girl that comes readily to mind, you can use this." He opened the magazine to the centerfold. "It's often more productive to have direct, visual stimulation at the point of orgasm." He handed me the Playboy and leaned back in his chair. "You have your climax, and note down how pleasurable it was. Then you come back and tell me about it."

"That's all?"

"That's all there is to it. Maybe nothing will happen—maybe you won't even ejaculate—we have to find this out. It's like a little experiment. But you probably will, and I want to know all about it."

"So at the point where I'm about to come, that's when I switch to the centerfold?"

"That's right. Piece of cake."

"Piece of cheesecake," I said.

"Ho!" Sly chortled. "Cheesecake! I like that! What a sense of humor!" he slapped his desk. "That's a good sign, Paul. Jesus loves a cheerful camper. With that attitude, you'll be on your way in no time!" He carefully put his cigar out by rolling the tip in the ashtray. "And uh, by the way, I'd just as soon you didn't flash that magazine around. Some folks think my treatments are a little unorthodox."

"Got it," I said. I left his office with the Playboy rolled up in my hand.

* * *

The guys slept in a modest bungalow next to the playing field, while Sheila stayed in the house. That night, after we turned out the lights, I figured I might as well do my homework. I pulled out the Playboy and a shaft of moonlight shone on the glossy pages. I'd just opened it to the centerfold when Jackson propped himself on his elbow in the next bed. "What's this?" he said, and tried to grab it. I held it back, but then thought what the hell, and showed him the magazine. "Whoa, you better not let the Rev see this. Where'd you get it?"

"He's the one who gave it to me."

"You be razzin' me, bro!"

"No, really." I told him about my homework.

"To think I been avoiding our next appointment. Jerking off for Jesus? Hell, I been doin' that all along!"

"Yeah, but then you got to look at this." I pointed at the centerfold.

"I know!" Jackson said, snapping his fingers. "I'll trade my mag for Sheila's. They probably got her a Playguy!"

Just then, Sly entered the bunkhouse and Jackson hid the magazine. Sometimes the Rev would "bunk with the boys" to keep us company and provide a suitable father figure. "Don't mind me," he said, but we pretended to be asleep. He stood by my bunk and took off all his clothes, then hopped buck naked on top of the next bed. He always said it's better not to have any unnecessary binding cut off the circulation of vital bodily fluids during the night. Once the Rev started snoring, I could hear Jackson squeaking in the next bunk, no doubt doing his homework.

10: Castro Scuffle

I had of course heard of cults who cut themselves off from outside contacts, but Escape wasn't like that. Sly didn't believe in sequestering us from the temptation of worldly influences. We were engaged in a real life battle for human souls that took us directly into the devil's trenches. In the face of actual combat, we would be forced to defend our faith, like iron being tempered into hardened steel.

After a few weeks of intense indoctrination, we "fledged"—confronting the damned in their lair. The Gay Pride Parade was our first outing, which was a great success. Afterwards, we watched the video. I especially liked the part where the Homo Nation boys got all riled up when I told them, "Jesus loves you." Even the Rev pointed out that such a strong response was an indication that I had pierced their defenses. "That was the devil kicking and screaming. You speared him in the side, Paul." Sly stroked my head and rested his hand on my shoulder.

I was more than willing to go along to witness for Jesus, because it meant I was part of something greater than myself. If anyone blocked our way, we were emboldened. If anyone argued with us, we would confront them with the Holy Writ. If we were spat upon, it only made us stronger and more determined to mount the barricades to God's Kingdom.

After our debut at the parade, we were all fired up. Sly gathered the troops for a pep rally every day after Bible Study. We made some more signs decrying the moral degeneration of the homosexual lifestyle. We printed up flyers inviting sinners to come to our prayer meetings. Sly even made up a comic book, which was quite explicit, spelling out in lurid detail the punishment awaiting those who groveled in lust and sodomy. I will always remember Sly's stern warning: "It's your choice—you will either be forged in the fire of righteousness, or burn in eternity!"

The only trouble was, even standing at the corner of Castro and 18th, the heart of gay San Francisco, we were mostly ignored—that is, until we met our match in the boys from Homo Nation, the feisty group that scorned us during the Gay Parade. By providing us with a clear antagonist, they transformed us from a motley crew of Christian do-gooders to a powerful threat to Satan's stronghold.

These scrappy dudes could not resist a fight. One day we were picketing the Castro Theater for showing For a Lost Soldier, this film about a Dutch boy being seduced by a Canadian infantryman during World War II. Jackson was dressed in his usual homeboy outfit. I wore jeans and a T-shirt, a big mistake, since it was freezing cold in the July fog. Sheila had put Sly's wool shirt over her summer dress, and Perry wore a suit. Ruth videotaped us as we marched in a circle in front of the theater, singing the "Battle Hymn of the Republic," and carrying signs that read: "The Heterosexual Solution—Spurn Sodomy!" "Save the Children!" "God Condemns Unnatural Affection," and "Heaven is for the Blessed, not the Sex-Obsessed!"

Interestingly, another small group was also picketing the theater: all women, dressed like typical dykes—overalls, work shirts, and buttons that read "Don't be a prick, we'll cut off your dick!" Two women carried a banner proclaiming themselves the Lesbian Revengers. They held up signs like "Boycott Child Seduction!" and "NABME Cannot Hide!" NABME refers to the North American Boy-Man Escapades, a notorious ring of child sex-traffickers.

Suddenly a band of Homo Nation types rushed down the street from the corner, blowing their whistles, yelling "We're here! We're queer! We're gonna have a party, and you're not invited!" They broke our signs and scattered our tracts on the ground. Sly tried to grab a sign that said "Jesus was a homo" from the guy who caught my eye at the gay parade, and got punched in the nose for his trouble.

The women were caught off guard, unsure whose side they were on. A rather burly-looking gal with short-cropped hair got into a yelling match about NABME with this same guy. "They're a bunch of child molesters!" she screamed.

"Yeah? When I was sixteen, I wanted it!"

"You self-oppressing fag!"

"Sex-negative hag!" Ready to scratch each others' eyes out, he suddenly recognized me over her shoulder. "Shame!" he cried, pointing at me.

His eyes sparking with passion, I could tell he was suffering from intense inner torment by the way he grimaced and gestured. His jaw with two days growth jutted into the air, his dark eyebrows knitted together, his arm raised, the bulge of his biceps peeking out of his T-shirt, he clenched his fist in a powerful demonstration of fury. This seemed like a crucial moment—I really wanted to make some kind of significant contact, but I was so struck by the anguish that so obviously consumed him, I was speechless.

Instantly united, Homo Nation and the Lesbian Revengers shook their fingers at us. "Shame! Shame! Shame!" they hissed, and advanced upon us menacingly.

We hastily gathered what was left of our scattered tracts and signs and fled toward Market. Sly led the retreat as epithets hurtled past our ears. I'll never forget the look of beatitude that graced his bloody face as we crossed the street and scampered down the steps to the Castro subway.

11: Here's Spit in Your Eye

When we got back to the ranch, the Rev could not let our rout rest. He was outraged, ranting about the lack of police protection and the violation of our First Amendment rights— freedom of speech, religion, and assembly. Luckily, Ruth had videotaped the entire attack, so we'd be able to identify the culprits, if it ever came to a lineup. Seeing ourselves on TV seemed more real somehow than when we were actually there. I wondered what it would be like to see a video of your life. Somehow it would make it seem more like it really happened. Of course mine would have to be edited for family audiences.

Sly spent the next few days trying to get the DA to file charges. He took the tape to City Hall, but they ignored him. He left each Supervisor a copy, but doubted they even looked at it. "One can never underestimate the power of the Homosexual Lobby," he declared. Finally, he wormed his way onto the agenda at the next Board of Supervisors meeting, where we'd have a chance to confront this travesty of justice.

We girded our loins for another sortie into the lion's den. At the meeting, Sly took the mike and denounced the brown-shirt tactics of these gay Nazis. Ruth ushered us into seats near the front of the hall. "This will be an excellent lesson in secular civics," she said.

"We're not an enemy to gays," Sly continued. "They have the prerogative to live however they please. Those people who claim they're happy, fine, go your own way. But we want to offer an alternative to those who are miserable about their condition, and who want out of the lifestyle."

"Why do you think they're unhappy?" a woman shouted. "It's 'cause of self-hating fags like you." She had a ring through her nose and no doubt bells on her toes. What a freak show.

Sly looked around furiously, but tried to stay calm. "It would be wrong to turn away from them in their hour of need. We are simply addressing the desires of those who genuinely want our help, and these brawlers and hoodlums have no right to disrupt our religious demonstration."

"That was no prayer meeting, buster, that was a hate rally!" a man shouted from the line that had formed to speak at the mike. I recognized him as my nemesis from Homo Nation.

"Go, Jimmy!" someone shouted.

Sly continued. "How ironic it is that these so-called civil libertarians allow abortionists to maim women's souls and murder innocent children, but they prohibit constitutional protest; they demand the right to pornography, pedophilia, and sodomy, but when it comes to hearing the Word of God they totally freak out."

"His time's up!" shouted another woman. I recognized her as the husky Lesbian Revenger from our scuffle on Castro Street. A bunch of queers and dykes started blowing their whistles.

The President of the Board banged the gavel and threatened to clear the auditorium unless everyone settled down. She asked Sly to step away from the mike, but then the next person in line gave his time to the Rev.

"No fair! He already got a chance to speak!"

The President ignored this outburst, so Sly continued his speech. "Special rights for homosexuals would be an injustice to those who struggled for civil rights in the sixties. This is a sick behavior, not a true minority! Blacks, animals, homos—what's next? Special rights for bestiality and pedophiles? Homosexuals don't need any special rights—why they already have a standard of living twice as high as the average heterosexual!"

"Bullshit!" shouted Jimmy. "What is this, a commie-fag-Jewish conspiracy? Why not gas us all!"

"What I'm saying," Sly continued, "is that the manipulation of the civil rights issue by immoral sexual deviants is an insult to the true minorities of this country!" He took his seat among hoots and jeers.

Then a black minister got up to the mike and reminded the audience that the NAACP passed a resolution supporting civil rights regardless of sexual orientation. "That means that you, too, would not be discriminated against, just because you're straight. And when, I would like to know, was the last time the Christian right stood up for black people? Where were you when the Ku Klux Klan strung up blacks in Mississippi and burned school busses in Alabama? Exactly who are the opportunists, here?"

Sly stormed up to the mike. "I have one more thing to say."

"Sit down!" yelled the nose-ring. "You already had your turn! No fair!" Whistles pierced the chamber, but Sly grabbed the mike from the other minister.

"The freedom train to Selma did not stop at Sodom!" Sly thundered.

As Sly left the microphone, Jimmy spit at him. Sly reeled backward, horrified and disgusted. "Did you see that?" Sly shouted, pointing at Jimmy. "He spat at me! You filthy slime, AIDS-spreading vermin. Assault! Assault and battery, with HIV! Arrest this man for intent to commit murder!" Following a brief scuffle, Jimmy was handcuffed and dragged off by the police, who wore their infamous yellow gloves.

"Your gloves don't match your shoes! Your gloves don't match your shoes!" shouted the homos, dykes, and queers, stomping and whistling.

Leaving the Supervisor's chambers, a flurry of news media crowded around Sly as he wiped his face with a handkerchief. Flashbulbs went off, and reporters thrust their microphones towards him. "Could you give us a statement, Reverend Slocock?"

"Are you going to press charges?"

"How does it feel to be persecuted, Reverend?"

He pressed his way through the crowd. Outside, he stood on the steps of City Hall and gave an impromptu press conference. "Homosexual rights, abortion on demand, women in combat boots, assaults on religious leaders—that's change all right, but not the kind of change we can abide in God's country."

"Reverend Slocock," asked one reporter, the videocameras whirring next to him, "do you object to being referred to as the Religious Right?"

"Do I mind being called the Religious Right?" The Rev broke into a huge grin. "Not at all. We're religious, aren't we? And we're right!" He struck his fist into the air. "No problemo."

He waved and walked down the steps in triumph, then we hustled him through the throng of jeering homos back to the van.

* * *

That night, I was so wound up from the events of the day, it was hard for me to get to sleep. I figured I might as well take a stab at my "homework." I tried to imagine someone like Matt from the Boy Scouts, my usual fantasy, but no matter how hard I tried, I kept thinking of Jimmy—Jimmy with his fierce scowl, Jimmy with his fist in the air, Jimmy with his tight shirt grabbing his muscles, his shorts swishing between his thighs, Jimmy being handcuffed and dragged away by the police. I got out the magazine and was all ready to turn to the centerfold, when I popped, thinking of Jimmy.

12: What a Friend I've Found in Jesus

On my way to my next counseling session, I ran into Jackson, who winked conspiratorially. "Doin' your homework?" he yelled.

"Get out of here," I said, and waved him on.

"Practice makes perfect!" He made an obscene stroking gesture and laughed like an idiot.

I was a little concerned about meeting with the Rev, knowing he expected me to give a full and accurate accounting of our little experiment. It wasn't something I felt very comfortable talking about, especially since it was such a dismal failure.

Of course, Sly wanted to know all the details. "I want to know exactly what happened, so I can assess your progress. It will also help you break free from the compulsion. So, first of all, who were you thinking about when you started touching yourself?"

"Some guy."

"Any particular guy?"

"Just a guy I knew in junior high."

"Did you ever see him naked?"

"Maybe once or twice."

"Where did you see him naked? In gym class?"

"On a campout. We were in the Boy Scouts."

"Was he well-built?"

"Pretty well-built. Not a muscle man, or anything. He was on the swim team."

"Broad shoulders, slim waist, well-developed pectorals?"

"I guess you could say so. He was very handsome. He had a great smile."

"Did you ever do anything sexual with this boy?"

"No."

Sly seemed disappointed. "Are you sure?"

"I think I'd remember," I said. He no doubt thought I was holding out on him.

"And as you came closer to the point of inevitability, did you switch to the pinup girl?"

"Well, I opened the magazine."

"Good, good. And then tell me what happened next."

"I came."

"You had an orgasm, stroking yourself and looking at the magazine?"

"Yes," I lied. I felt the color rise in my cheeks.

"There's no reason to be embarrassed," he said. "Good work!"

For some reason, I couldn't bring myself to tell him that even though I had opened the magazine, I was still thinking of a guy—not even about Matt, but about Jimmy, who had just spit in his face at the Board of Supervisors meeting. But I figured it would just add insult to injury, and I didn't want to hurt his feelings.

Although this was supposed to be about my recovery, and how was I going to make any progress if I lied to my spiritual counselor?

"There was something else," I said.

"What's that?" Sly asked, leaning close.

"Well, I uh..." suddenly I lost my nerve.

"Speak up, son."

"I, uh, showed Jackson the magazine. I'm sorry, I know you said not to tell anyone, but I thought maybe he could use the help."

Sly laughed. "That's perfectly all right. It was a Christian impulse, and I'm proud of you!" He got up from his chair, and patted my back. "Now, the next step is to show you a videotape while I read some suggestions about your experience. But before we start, you need to take this pill." He held up a white capsule.

"A pill? What's that supposed to do?"

"It induces unpleasant associations with your homosexual inclinations. You may find yourself getting aroused at first, and then experience some other feelings as we go along. Don't fight against your natural impulses."

He handed me the pill, but I must have looked at it with some misgivings.

"Trust me," he said, and squeezed my shoulder.

I took the pill. He offered me a glass of water, and put a plastic-lined trash receptacle next to me, "just in case."

"Just in case of what?" I asked.

"You'll see." He dimmed the lights, and turned on the VCR.

"I want you to imagine that you are in a room with this handsome young man," he read.

On the screen appeared a well-built guy, turned slightly away from the camera. I could see his back and his buttocks, his face in profile.

"He is completely naked."

He turned toward me, and I could see his well-built chest and biceps, slim waist, his genitals in shadow. As the camera zoomed in on him, he turned into the light and began to get an erection. (So did I, to tell you the truth.) This was pretty hot, but I couldn't imagine how this was supposed to help me get over it. I looked over at Sly to see if he was sure this was the right tape.

He directed me back to watching the video. "As you approach him, you notice that he has sores and lesions all over his body, with pus oozing from his scabs."

It was really disgusting—all of a sudden, his body became a mottled patchwork of sores that multiplied and spread all over his skin—down his arms, across his chest, onto his genitals.

I heard Sly break open a capsule off to the side. A close-up on the screen showed hideous sores spread all across the man's face.

"A terrible foul stench comes from his body. The odor is so strong it makes you sick."

The man's face twisted in pain and horror. I smelled rotten eggs. Suddenly I felt a wave of nausea flood through my body.

"You begin to feel food particles coming up in your throat."

I grabbed the wastebasket.

"You can't help yourself and you vomit all over the place—over the floor, on your hands and clothes, and the nauseous smell makes you even sicker, and you vomit all over everything."

I fell out of the chair on my knees and heaved into the basket again and again. Having emptied myself, I continued to have dry heaves until all I could taste was bitter bile at the end of each spasm.

Sly rubbed my back and pressed a moist washcloth to my forehead. He gave me a glass of water. I rinsed my mouth and spat it out, then drank the rest. I immediately heaved again. Faint with exhaustion and dripping with sweat, my stomach continued to spasm and cramp. My head was pounding and I could barely move. I propped myself on the edge of the wastebasket. He gave me some tissues and I wiped my mouth. "Good job," he said. "Suffering in the service of the Lord."

Somehow, I wasn't quite as enthused as he was. You bastard, I thought, but was too exhausted to say so. What a friend I'd found in Jesus.

* * *

Painful as this ordeal was, later on I started thinking that maybe it had worked. It was difficult for me to think of that naked guy getting a hard-on without wanting to puke. I couldn't get the odor of rotten eggs mixed with vomit out of my head. All sexual feelings had left me—even the idea of doing my "homework" didn't appeal to me in the least. Perhaps I'd been released from this agony once and for all.

13: To the Street Called Straight

Each member of our group was given the task of coming up with some form of outreach, which was designed not only to save other souls, but to shore up our own faith and commitment to reorientation. It was based on the concept, "Each one reach one," which, if successful, would expand exponentially throughout the world and result in the conversion of almost everyone in time for the Rapture.

Though such a long-range task seemed gargantuan, it was important to keep focused on the small contribution that each of us could make. Jackson figured he could just as easily witness for Jesus while building a pyramid empire by selling water filters. He recruited Sheila and Perry to be his first reps.

I, rather stupidly, was less smitten by entrepreneurial prospects, and instead wanted to take on a real spiritual challenge by confronting the devil in his lair, as Sly had so intriguingly put it. I told the Rev I wanted to visit Jimmy, the young man who spit on him at the Board of Supervisors meeting. Having no money for bail, he still languished in the County Jail at 850 Bryant Street. I thought his lonely sojourn might have given him time to reflect on his evil past, and that he would be ripe for the consoling influence of our Saviour.

Sly was skeptical at first. It violated two of our most fundamental rules—not to go off by ourselves, and certainly not to San Francisco. But in the end, he decided that I had made sufficient progress in my own rehabilitation to risk such an encounter. Besides, inmates were only allowed one visitor at a time.

"It is a generous act to reach out to reprobates who have scorned you. In your heart, you must realize that those who treat us with the utmost contempt are often the ones most vulnerable to our message. Just as Saul was struck blind on the road to Damascus, so that he might know the Truth, so may you strike fear into this recalcitrant youth. 'And the Lord said, "Rise and go, to the street called Straight,"' and let the scales fall from his eyes."

So I set off on my journey to the Sin City jail, full of compassion and eager anticipation. I boarded the bus for San Francisco, and watched the fog swirl among the cables stretched high above us on the Golden Gate Bridge. As we approached the city, I felt excited, but nervous. Would I be able to stand up to his cynical questions? Could I stay focused, not reacting out of anger or fear? As I approached the cement block structure at Eighth and Bryant, my heart was pumping in my chest, my palms sweaty. I tried to keep in mind what Sly had said: "The Goal is the Soul."

We waited in line to give our names while people were let in a few at a time to visit. We had to provide the name of the prisoner we wished to see. Luckily I had found Jimmy's last name in the newspaper the day after our skirmish at the Board of Supervisors, little realizing I might some day confront him face to face.

People of every color, in all shapes and dress, crowded the corridor: a woman with a black eye and three small children; a dark-skinned man wearing a turban; a woman in a wheel chair; an older woman carrying a pink box that smelled like an apple pie—which, of course, would have to be left behind, as they would never let a package from the outside world inside the jail.

Finally, my name was called. Visitors had to go through a metal detection unit, but we weren't searched. I was given a number, and found my cubicle. It had a thick glass window separating me from the prisoner's booth. We could only communicate by phone—no physical contact was allowed. A guard brought out a dark-haired young man dressed in orange overalls with short sleeves. He took one look at me and scowled. He turned away, but the guard shoved him back in the booth. He picked up the phone. "Who are you and what do you want?" he demanded.

His dark eyebrows formed a jagged line across his forehead, his slate-blue eyes electric and penetrating. My breath was taken away, and I nearly forgot what I had come for. "My name is Paul," I said. "We've never actually met, but I've seen you a couple of times."

"You were at the Supervisors meeting, with that asshole preacher."

"Plus the demo at the Castro theater. And the parade," I added.

"The parade?"

"I was the one who yelled, 'Jesus loves you.'"

He rolled his eyes and shook his head. "Oh, jeez. Another holy roller. You people could care less about me—all you want is another notch in your Bible. You think homos are going to hell, end of discussion, down on your knees."

I decided to let this provocation slide.

"So what's next? Do I know the Lord, Jesus? Have I been saved? Washed by the blood of the lamb?"

"Well, yes," I said. "I think it would help. John 3:36 tells us, 'He who believes in the Son has eternal life.'"

"You want to talk religion? I'll talk religion—but only if you're willing to take the stick out of your butt and say how you really feel."

"Try me," I said.

"As if half of you weren't queer as a three dollar bill."

"That's true," I said, "we are. Or we were. We're part of an ex-gay ministry."

"Oh, brother," he clunked the side of his head. "I don't believe this. Another bunch of self-hating fags. That is the worst. At least Jehovah's Witnesses don't know any better."

I wasn't sure what to say to that. All that came to mind were some testimonials from our HomoAnon meeting, like "Homosexuality is inherently repulsive."

"Not to me, it ain't."

"It's a false identity."

"What's your true identity?" he countered. "The closet? Denial? Self-hatred?"

"It's crooked at its basic root," I said.

"It works for me."

"There's an emptiness at the heart of homosexuality."

"Who are you fooling?" he said. "It isn't anyone but yourself."

This sounded so much like Sly that I became confused. "'Watch therefore, for you do not know on what day your Lord is coming,'" I reminded him.

"Oh, we're quoting scripture, are we?" he said. "'Beware of false prophets, who come to you in sheep's clothing but inwardly are ravenous wolves.'"

"Homosexual acts are against the will of God," I said.

"Says who?"

"Leviticus, for one: 'Thou shalt not lie with a man as with a woman—it is an abomination!'"

"'You hypocrite!'" he said, pointing at me. "'First take the log out of your own eye, and then you will see clearly to take the speck out of your brother's eye.'"

"That's what we're trying to do!" I said. My heart was beating fast, and I felt my face flushed by our scriptural duel. "Remember Sodom and Gomorrah, destroyed by fire and brimstone!"

"Oh yeah? Remember the pink triangle!"

I wavered a bit at this reference to Nazi Germany. Surely he didn't believe good Christians could ever condone concentration camps—even for gays. "This is about salvation, not politics," I said.

"The Religious Right is hardly what I'd call 'apolitical,'" he countered.

"'Neither the immoral nor thieves nor homosexuals will enter the Kingdom of God,'" I reminded him.

"'Judge not, lest ye yourself be judged,'" he said.

"'Their women exchanged natural relations for unnatural,'" I quoted, "'and the men likewise gave up natural relations with women and were consumed with passion for one another.'"

As I said this, he pressed himself against the window, clawing the glass and moaning.

"'Men committing shameless acts with men…'" I continued, but then watching him writhe against the glass, I lost my train of thought and couldn't finish the verse. "See how you are!" I said. I was shocked at this provocative display, yet strangely aroused.

He pulled his lips away from the glass and held the receiver to his mouth. "'Receiving in their own persons the due penalty for their error,'" he said, finishing the quote. "'Beloved, let us love one another; for love is of God, and he who loves is born of God and knows God.'"

"'The wages of sin is death!'" I exclaimed.

Jimmy sat down again and spoke into the phone while he glared at me. "Well did Isaiah prophesy of you hypocrites, as it is written, 'This people honors me with their lips, but their heart is far from me; in vain do they worship me, teaching as doctrines the precepts of men.'"

Then we both fell silent. He stared at me with his piercing eyes, and I looked away, feeling troubled. Unrepentant sinner that he was, I still admired his fierceness. Plus he obviously had been brought up with the Bible, which I'd barely even cracked. I was clearly out of my league and grasping at straws. Besides, I'd run out of Scriptures.

The guard came by. "Two minutes. Wrap it up."

"Tell you what," Jimmy said. "When I get out of this joint, I'll come to your ranch, or Bible camp, or whatever the hell it is. We can 'rap' some more about Scripture, if you like."

"Would you?" I asked, then tried not to seem overly eager. I didn't want him to feel pressured. I quickly gave him directions to Escape.

"I'm not promising anything, but I'd like to tell that homophobe Reverend a thing or two."

* * *

I left the jail, feeling oddly humiliated, yet charged and excited. I could tell he wasn't really a bad sort. It was obvious that he was a Christian, only he'd been tempted and fallen, as all of us had. Sly was right—Jimmy was ripe for picking. I would pray for guidance, and study hard to confront him again. If I was patient, he would drop into my palm. What a sweet plum for Jesus!

14: The Peter Meter

The night after I saw Jimmy, I dreamt I was at the jail again, talking to him on the phone, only we were both naked. Jimmy pressed himself against the glass, his lips open, his tongue smearing the window. As much as I tried to pull away, I felt drawn toward the glass. The cold, transparent divider kept us apart, but then as we writhed against the glass, it became liquid and slippery, yielding yet still dividing. I could almost feel us touching, and I ejaculated against the window.

I came with such force I woke myself up, my shorts gooey. I squirmed against the bed with the last spasm, trying to hold onto this feeling of intense pleasure, then suddenly grew cold and ashamed. To think that I had sexually objectified the very person I was trying to convert! I was horrified. But then I remembered how the Rev had warned me that Satan would not willingly release me from his talons—"Just remember, those dark, delicious desires are not coming from you. They're temptations from the devil!"

That's right! I felt the power of darkness seething in my soul. I pulled off my stained shorts and flung them on the floor. What a devious, sinister demon! To sully the noble intention of my efforts to bring another soul to Jesus in such a foul and dastardly fashion! What was it that Sly told me to say? "Get thee behind me, Satan!" That's right!

"Get thee behind me, Satan!" I shouted.

"Huh?" Jackson's sleepy voice asked. "Whazzat?"

"Oh, sorry, Jackson. It's nothing. Go back to sleep." Perry slept right through my outburst, and luckily Sly wasn't with us that night. I turned on my side, feeling purged, and tried to go back to sleep, full of fitful dreams, images of bats flying out of caves, horned silhouettes dancing against the flames.

*　　*　　*

The next day, I had another appointment with the Rev. I felt too sheepish to describe the exact nature of my dream, but I told myself I would cooperate with whatever task he set me. There would be nothing too arduous, no ocean too wide, no mountain too steep to keep me away from my destiny.

I told him about my meeting with Jimmy. "He said he had a thing or two to say to you, as well," I warned him.

Sly lay a finger to the side of his nose. "He wants to come here, does he?"

I nodded, eager, yet uncertain about his reply.

"I don't know. The progress that all of you are making is so fragile."

"I think there's a lot at stake here. Jimmy knows the Bible. He has fallen, it's true, and is full of contempt, but like you said, he is all the more vulnerable because of his sharp reactions."

"He's a sly one, that Jimmy. I'm not sure I trust him."

"But he's on the verge of truth!" I blurted out.

"He is, is he?" Sly said. "I sense a keen interest in you for this young man's salvation."

My face burned. Was I that transparent? Perhaps it would be better to confess my struggle, but then I feared Sly would keep Jimmy away. It might make it easier for me if he did. But I knew Jimmy was so close to salvation, that I could not risk his loss just to gratify my own need to escape temptation. It would not be fair to him, so I kept silent.

Sly then introduced my next treatment. "It's called Aversive Therapy. The idea is to attach an unpleasant feeling to a pleasant stimulus, in this case, a homosexual fantasy."

After my previous ordeal, I had some foreboding about submitting myself to an even more aversive remedy. But then I remembered my vow to confront my demons, and went along cheerfully. Sly led me to a small screening room down the hall from his office, which had a comfortable lounge chair, upholstered in black vinyl, facing a white screen. On the arm was a hand-held device which resembled a VCR remote-control. An electric transformer stood next to the chair with a loop of wire coming out of it. The room was stifling hot, almost like a sauna.

Sly lifted the wire, which ended in a small circle. "This wire is connected to the plethysmograph. It measures the level of arousal experienced by the subject when shown certain slides."

I was trying to fathom how this little wire was going to detect my arousal. "What's a plethysmograph?"

"The plethysmograph is basically a peter meter," he explained. "You slip this elastic loop around your penis—" I must have had a pained expression, because he hastily added, "don't worry, it won't constrict the blood flow. Then you'll be shown some slides of naked men. If you get an erection, you'll be given an electric shock."

Oh, my God, I thought. This is medieval.

"It's just a mild shock. Somewhat unpleasant, but entirely harmless. The transformer is set at the lowest voltage." Here he pointed out the different buttons on the remote-control. "With this remote, you'll have complete control over how long you look at the slide. This button blanks the screen. If you stare at the naked man longer than seven seconds, you'll get a shock regardless of whether you get a hard-on. So don't get caught fantasizing about these hunky guys, or you'll get your dick zapped.

"This button replaces the men with slides of naked women. You can stare at these women for as long as you like. While ogling these voluptuous vixens, you can even get aroused, and you won't get shocked."

Then he showed me some other features he had built into the room. "With the female slides, some nice music will come on, and a little air conditioning."

I thought that would help, as I was already sweating.

"The sound of a babbling brook will soothe you. If you want, while looking at the females, you can even masturbate. Just use those tissues when you come, and don't get any jism on the wires or it'll cause a short."

He had me sit in the chair and adjust it until I was comfortable. He said he would leave the room while I put the band around my penis, and sit in the control booth to gauge the proper circumference of a flaccid fit. Then he would show the first slide, and the treatment would begin.

"The idea is that you'll eventually come to associate the male nude with anxiety and pain. When a man has been conditioned to hate and fear his homosexuality, his re-orientation to heterosexuality can be a very great relief."

Somehow I did not find this entirely reassuring.

"Just remember, you're in complete control. If you switch to the female slides as soon as you feel the slightest arousal, you don't have to get shocked at all." He patted me on the shoulder, and left the room.

I carefully put on the elastic band, and was relieved that I was not in the least bit excited in anticipating this experiment. In fact, I felt downright queasy, especially after my previous nauseating treatment. Still, I wasn't convinced that I would be in complete control of whether or not I got shocked. I've never felt as though I had any influence, much less clout, over my arousal—my penis always seemed to have a mind of its own. In the middle of geometry, it would suddenly spring up at an acute angle for no reason at all. To say nothing of the showers after gym class, when I had to avert my eyes and think of algebra equations to keep from popping a boner.

While in the midst of these thoughts, the first slide appeared on the screen—the torso of a handsome guy springing out of the water, the lower part of his body covered by the spray. That was pretty easy—I just looked at it for a few seconds, and then blanked the screen with nary a twinge.

The next slide was a naked man riding on horseback through the woods. His hair flew in the wind as he crouched under a branch, his muscular thighs gripping the horse's flanks. It was like a nature photo, and I could appreciate his physique just as I appreciated the horse's body as a work of muscle in motion. No problem. I blanked the screen.

A photo came up of a man drying himself off, the leg nearest me up on a bench, just the tip of his penis peaking out from underneath. Other naked figures in the background were blurred by the steam. I felt the slightest tingle, and immediately blanked the screen. I decided to replace it with a woman to cool off a bit. So far, so good—no shocks.

The woman was propped up on some pillows. She had long hair, and a sweet smile. Her breasts rose like mounds, crested by dark nipples. The music came on and a cool mist blew gently into the room. I relaxed for a minute, then hit the button for the next slide.

This one was full frontal nudity of a muscular young man standing on a boulder by a rushing stream, staring straight at the camera. Dark hair fell across his eyes. He looked serious, but pleasant, and had such tender lips. Before I even realized what was happening, I felt a zap to my groin. I dropped the remote, and it kept zapping me. I wriggled in my seat to reach the damn device while experiencing these god-awful jolts. "Yow!" I yelled. I finally grabbed the remote and blanked the screen. What a relief. I looked down, expecting to find the charred remains of my former self. Luckily, I was quite intact, shriveled but unharmed. I figured I'd better keep the remote in my lap, not on the arm of the chair, and clicked the button for another female.

This woman had long brown hair, her tongue touching her lip as she caressed her breasts. The babbling brook and cool mist again relaxed me. I tried touching myself, but my penis was unresponsive, a limp noodle.

The next slide showed two naked men in profile, kissing sweetly. One had his hand on the other's chest, while the other grasped the small of his back. Their partial erections, silhouetted against the dark background, barely grazed each other. I quickly blanked the screen.

Next, a man sat on a bed, leaning one arm on his raised knee, cupping his balls with his other hand. Since he was facing head on, it took me a moment to realize he had an erection. I tried to blank the screen as soon as I recognized it, but it was too late—zapped again.

Another woman. The cool mist, the soothing music. The dark triangle of hair parted by her fingers to reveal the moist, pink inner lips of her vagina. I tried to work up some enthusiasm for entering her mysterious depths, but it didn't work. I wasn't repelled or put off; just indifferent.

Another slide, this time a man licking the head of an erect cock while stroking his own penis. I felt a sudden deep yearning, and could not tear my eyes away even as the electric shock pulsed through my own erection. The elastic band worked its way up my expanding penis until it stimulated the area just below the head. Riveted to this image of an aroused man going down on his lover, I felt the fullness of my rock-hard cock vibrate and twitch with each zap of current until I spurted at the screen.

*   *   *

I must have lost consciousness. The screen was blank, and the fluorescent lights came on. The Rev turned off the transformer. I shyly unhooked the elastic band and zipped myself up. Too embarrassed even to apologize for the mess, I started wiping the vinyl with tissues.

Sly occupied himself by fiddling with the wires. "This wasn't supposed to happen. I'm not sure what went wrong. I'm going to have to check the voltage on that damn thing. It's not supposed to electrocute you!"

I was relieved that he chose to ignore my discomfort. "Can I go now?" I asked.

"Sure, sure. We'll talk again tomorrow. See you at vespers."

15: Fruit of the Loom

Fellowshipping was a happy time at Escape. Everyone gathered around the piano in the Fireside Room and Sly pounded out inspirational songs, such as "You Are My Hiding Place, Oh Lord." It was like an old-fashioned revival meeting, but still had a family feel to it, since we'd all come to know each other pretty well. Over the weeks and months, we'd become familiar with each other's idiosyncrasies and genuine gifts from the Lord. Perry always had an insightful angle to add to scriptural doctrine. Sheila was on the look-out for women's interests. And Jackson, especially, excelled at injecting a joyous note into our festivities, which if left to Ruth and Sly tended toward solemn and serious.

Every night after some reading from the Scriptures and an inspirational talk by Sly or Ruth, Jackson would lead us in a call and response. We'd clap our hands, stomp our feet, and sing out praises to the glory of the Lord:

"Clap your hands and sing it for the Lord! (all together now)"

"Coming 'round for Jesus!"

"Lift your eyes to Heaven above—"

"We'll sing, 'Glory Hallelujah!'"

There was something comforting about having our days spelled out for us, and then coming together to celebrate our love for Jesus, our sense of family, and our gratitude for being saved from a life of sin and sorrow. Once in a while I'd wonder what it would be like to leave the ranch and go out on my own again, and I'd get to feeling kind of wistful—as much as I sometimes yearned to be released from some of the arbitrary rules, I genuinely liked the structure, the sense of belonging, and the fellowship with my fellow campers.

It was strange, even paradoxical in a way, but I used to feel like such a freak for being gay. Coming here, and meeting other gays for the first time outside of a sexually-charged atmosphere, I began to realize that we're just people, like anyone else. We have a problem, no doubt—that's why we're here—and yet I began, ever so gradually, to feel better about myself. Almost more accepting of who I am, fundamentally, inside.

Not that I had any intention of becoming complacent—my treatment fiascoes had taught me considerable humility on that score. And my struggle with the Devil was going full tilt, with the final results by no means guaranteed ahead of time. Still, in the midst of our gospel songs, looking at Sheila's shining face, Sly pounding the piano, Perry shyly keeping time with his foot, and even Ruth getting a glow around the gills, I felt comforted and reassured that for the first time in my life, I genuinely belonged somewhere.

After our songfest, sometimes the four of us would put on a skit representing some scene from the Bible. That night, we decided to enact a tableau from the Immaculate Conception.

Sheila was Mary, of course. Perry played the angel Gabriel, and Jackson played Joseph. I scripted the scene from the Bible along with a few improvisations and narrated the show. Mary sat spinning some wool, waiting for Joseph to come home from work. We dressed Perry in a gown left by Francine's Beauty College, and made wings out of wire hangers and tissue. We fashioned Jackson a beard out of yarn, and he wore Sly's bathrobe.

Narrator: The angel Gabriel was sent from God to a city of Galilee named Nazareth, to a virgin betrothed to a man whose name was Joseph, of the house of David; and the Virgin's name was Mary.

Gabriel (offstage, loudly): Mary!

Mary (spinning wool, looks up, startled): Hark! Who goes there?

Gabriel (enters): Hail, O favored one, the Lord is with you!

Mary (looking troubled): What sort of greeting is this?

Gabriel: Do not be afraid, Mary, for you have found favor with God. And behold, you will conceive in your womb and bear a son, and you shall call his name Jesus.

Mary: How can that be, since I have no husband?

Gabriel: The Holy Spirit will come upon you. For with God, nothing will be impossible. Blessed are you among women, and blessed is the fruit of thy womb. Zap! You're pregnant!

[Exit, Gabriel]

Mary: O Lord, what shall I tell Joseph when he discovers that I am with child?

Narrator: A little while later—

Joseph (enters): What's this I hear, you be with child? I ask you, how can this be, since we ain't never even been together?

Mary: It was Gabriel, who came to me—

Joseph: Gabriel! That rat! Wait till I whack him upside the head—

Mary: It's not what you think—

Joseph: What am I supposed to think?

Mary: He's an angel!

Joseph: What is it with you, wench? Holding out on me to "save" yourself for the wedding night, when all this time you been diddling some rich Pharisee punkster.

Mary: No, I mean, he really is an angel. Sent by God!

Joseph: Yeah, right, and I'm the Holy Ghost.

Mary: No, it was the Holy Ghost that zapped me!

Joseph: The Holy Ghost made you pregnant?

Mary: Yes, He did!

Joseph: You really think I'm that gullible? You been fooling around, you get knocked up, and now you claim some ghost made you pregnant?

Mary: Yes! Yes! A thousand times, yes!

Joseph: What is this, the Immaculate Conception?

Mary: That's it! [snaps her fingers] I knew there was a name for it. My cousin Elizabeth—it happened to her, too!

Joseph: That tramp! What a fabrication! Maybe her husband bought that cockamamy line, but you ain't pulling no fruit of the loom over my eyes! I'm calling off the engagement! [Joseph stomps out.]

Mary: Oh, Lord, please show Joseph the Light and the Way! [weeping, exits]

Narrator: Being a just man and unwilling to put Mary to shame, to say nothing of having her stoned to death, Joseph resolved to divorce her quietly. But as he considered this, behold, an angel of the Lord appeared to him in a dream:

[Joseph enters, lies down. Gabriel enters with a clap of thunder—Narrator wiggles cookie sheet.]

Gabriel: Joseph!

Joseph: Huh? Whozzat?

Gabriel: I'm Gabriel, an angel sent from the Lord your God.

Joseph: [scrambling away from him] Ain't no angel gonna lay his hands on me!

Gabriel: Joseph, son of David, do not fear to make Mary your wife, for that which is conceived in her is of the Holy Spirit; she will bear a Son, and you shall call His name Jesus, for He will save His people from their sins. [exits]

Joseph (waking up, stretches, yawns): Oh, I had one weird dream! [shakes his head, exits]

Narrator: And so Joseph returned to Mary, to tell her of his prescient vision:

[Mary enters, spinning.]

Joseph (enters): Mary, forgive me, for I have been with an angel.

Mary: That slut! You pig! [She flies at him in her fury.]

Joseph (fending off her blows): No, no, I ain't never slept with no angel. But he told me your cock-and-bull story was true!

Mary (relenting): Praise be to the Lord! [They embrace.]

Narrator: The end. Well, it's not really the end—it's only the start of the New Beginning. Amen.

Ruth and Sly clapped. The four of us came back out, linked hands, and took a bow.

Sly shook our hands to congratulate us. "That was just fine. Wasn't that fine, Ruth?"

"Well, you certainly took some liberties with the Holy Writ," she replied, "but I would say you managed to capture the right spirit. That's what counts." Then she kissed me on the cheek.

16: The Curse of Canaan

Sly often disappeared for hours at a time, working on a new concept, he said, that would transform reorientation therapy forever. We were sort of curious, as he had postponed many of our sessions. But whenever we came around to his office, he'd chase us away. "Out! Out! Out! It's not ready yet. Now shoo!"

Ruth put Sheila in charge of running the kitchen. She oversaw meal preparation, including grocery shopping and menu planning. Although Sheila made a concerted effort, cooking appeared not to be her strongest suit. After a steady diet of Spam, fish sticks and tater tots, with lime Jello and tiny marshmallows for dessert, Perry rebelled and took charge of the kitchen.

This was a great relief, and the rest of us quickly fell in line under his culinary direction. Knowing that Ruth and Sly would not entirely approve of Perry and Sheila's role-reversal, we made sure that Sheila got all the credit for planning and cooking our meals.

"Isn't Sheila becoming the little homemaker?" Sly said one evening after a particularly fine repast. Perry had concocted a delicious cocque au vin, steaming corn bread, and a Caesar salad. Then, the piece de resistance, a home-made apple pie with a great flaky crust for dessert.

"She'll make some lucky man a dutiful and obedient wife," Ruth said.

Sheila blushed. "Thank you," she said. "It was really nothing."

Perry sat quietly, his hands folded, ready for our evening prayer. He seemed content to avoid the limelight, since he was happy as a clam planning the menus and telling us all what to do behind the scenes. Besides, he made sure that Jackson and I did most of the chopping, prep, and scouring up afterwards.

The conspiratorial quality of our cooperation contributed to the camaraderie of our little group, as we genuinely tried to look out for one another's interests. So long, of course, as our peccadillos did not substantially impinge on the longer-range goal of healing our sexual brokenness.

*   *   *

We continued to meet with Ruth in our Bible sessions, which over time grew more contentious. Ruth got noticeably rankled whenever we strayed far afield from the topic of homosexuality, but I think she tolerated our wide-ranging discussions because she hoped not only to free us from unnatural passion, but also to save our souls for eternity.

Ruth seemed to take a special interest in my "proficiency at exegesis," as she put it. This rather surprised me, as Perry far excelled my minimal knowledge of Scriptural passages. But she was often as not annoyed at the fine points Perry picked with her. One day he pointed out the contradiction between the story of the Prodigal Son being welcomed home in Luke 15, but a rebel son was stoned to death in Deuteronomy. "Then Exodus 21:17 says, 'Whoever curses his father or mother shall be put to death.'"

"What's a 'prodigal son?'" I asked.

"A boy who takes his inheritance, spurns his father's guidance, and goes off on his own," Perry explained. "He totally squanders his fortune with loose living, then comes crawling back. And his father forgives him, much to the annoyance of his brother, who was good all along."

I said, "Well, is that because the New Testament is supposed to be more forgiving?" Then I quoted a verse I'd come across in Second Corinthians: "The old has passed away, behold, the new has come."

Ruth turned to me and smiled. "Your question indicates a freshness of mind, an innocence, and a purity of faith that surpasseth understanding."

She gazed at me through her thick glasses as she brushed away a wayward strand of hair that had released itself from her tight bun.

Then she turned to the group and said, "That's enough for today, I should think. We'll continue again tomorrow."

The next day, Jackson was particularly worked up over this quote from Exodus 21:20: "'When a man strikes a slave, male or female, with a rod and the slave dies under his hand, he shall be punished. But if the slave survives a day or two, he is not to be punished; for the slave is his money.' So it's all right to kill a slave, as long as he doesn't die right away? I can't believe this!"

"Yes, well, we have to understand that in those days, slaves were considered private property," Ruth explained.

"But this is supposed to be the word of God!" Jackson said.

"Of course God knew slavery was wrong. But the people weren't ready to give it up."

Then Perry piped in. "Listen to Ephesians 6:5: 'Slaves, be obedient to those who are your earthly masters, with fear and trembling, in singleness of heart, as to Christ.'"

Ruth flinched. "Sometimes you have to live with certain inequities until the time is ripe."

"God didn't give Sodom and Gomorrah much slack," Sheila said.

"But that was an abomination," Perry pointed out.

Jackson looked at Perry in astonishment. "And slavery's not?"

"Well, look at Genesis 9:25: Noah said, 'Cursed be Canaan; a slave of slaves shall he be to his brothers.'"

"Why was Canaan cursed?" I asked.

Perry said, "Because his father, Ham, discovered Noah naked one night after he got drunk. He told his brothers, who then covered him up without looking at him."

Jackson shook his head. "Let me get this straight. Noah cursed Ham's son, Canaan, and condemned him to slavery because Ham found Noah drunk and naked?"

Perry nodded. "That's right."

Sheila said, "That's ridiculous! Noah went on a bender, tore off his clothes, and passed out. Why was it Ham's fault he found him naked? And worse yet, why should Ham's son be punished? Deuteronomy 24:16 says, 'The fathers shall not be put to death for the children, nor shall the children be put to death for the father.'"

Perry said, "But Exodus 20:4 says, 'for I the Lord your God am a jealous God, visiting the iniquity of the fathers upon the children to the third and the fourth generation of those who hate me.'"

"This is so bizarre!" Jackson said. "Why's it such a big deal Noah's son seen him naked? Then he cursed his grandson, Canaan, and that's how the southern states justified slavery? Tell me we're living on the same planet!"

17: Dangerous Liaison

After Bible study, these and other quandaries were swirling through my mind, when who should I see crossing the quad but a young man wearing baggy shorts, combat boots, a tight black T-shirt and a cap turned backwards?

"Jimmy!" I cried, and ran to his side. "When did you get out?"

He grinned at me. "Told you I'd come and visit. Didn't think I'd do it, did you?"

He told me the assault charges against him had been dismissed. Since saliva is not a vector for HIV transmission, spitting could not be considered a lethal weapon. "I'm not HIV positive, anyway, but I wouldn't let them test me because it was irrelevant."

I laughed, for no particular reason.

"What's so funny?"

"I don't know; just feeling good-humored, I guess. It's great to see you!"

Then he took me by the shoulders and looked me in the eye. "So, are you still a 'former homo?'"

I was startled by such a direct question, as if he had known me for a long time. Yet I was the one who had taken it upon myself to convert him. It was hard for me to meet his eyes, and I looked shyly away. "Well, I'm doing my best. It doesn't necessarily come all at once."

"'Come all at once'?" he grinned.

I blushed. "I admit, there are still urges, but you have to understand that's just the devil's influence."

He released my shoulders. "You really believe in all that Satan crap?"

"It's not from me!" I said, more emphatically than I intended.

"The devil made you do it, is that it?"

Then I got mad. "You can make all the fun you want, but on the day of Judgment, you won't be the one who's laughing all the way to hell!"

"Whoa, calm down, sport!" Jimmy punched me in the arm. "I'm just trying to understand where you're coming from."

I almost forgot myself. Here I'm trying to convert him, and I let him get so easily under my skin. That'll be the very thing that drives him away. "I'm sorry," I said. "Obviously it's still a struggle for me."

Just then, Jackson walked by us, wide-eyed and chomping on an apple. "Apple core," he yelled.

"Baltimore!" I yelled back.

"Who's the hunkster?" He arched his eyebrow and smirked.

I hesitated for a second, then shouted his name: "Jimmy!"

Jackson threw the core. Jimmy dodged it, laughing, then made as if to chase Jackson, who scampered off, grinning like a fool. "Mum's the word!"

I turned to Jimmy. "Does the Reverend know you're here?"

"No, thought I'd look around, check it out, then give him a piece of my mind."

"You're not staying?" I said.

"Staying? Here?" He stared at me as if I were a lunatic.

I didn't say anything, just looked at the ground as we walked toward the woods. I wondered why he came by, then; but I didn't want to ask because that would probably bring an end to our conversation and I'd never see him again.

He took my arm as we walked along. This felt a little intimate, to say nothing of unmanly, but I could not bear to pull away from him. I felt my penis jerk awake from its slumber, and stuffed my hand in my pocket.

"Listen, I realize my reputation precedes me," he said in this oddly literary tone. He pulled on the dried stalks of wild oats as we entered the live oaks and bay laurels at the edge of the playing field. "It would no doubt be presumptuous of me to assume your friendship. But I've come to see you as an inspiration."

I must have looked a little suspicious. He said, "I would never claim to be oblivious to how cute you are, but your physical beauty is not what really attracted me—it's your goodness and innocence that have won me over."

Here he paused to gauge how his words were affecting me, which I attempted to hide as best I could. I felt thrilled to hear that he found me attractive, even though it was against God's law. Then I felt ashamed to hear it was my supposed "goodness" that he felt inspired by—if he only knew how many nights I'd spent enthralled by his image while touching myself in ungodly ways!

He stopped and furrowed his dark brow in an effort to express himself. "Even though you knew about my past, and saw how much I disdained your beliefs, you were the only one who came to visit me in jail. It goes to show who your real friends are."

He looked at me with this incredible vulnerability, and my heart went out to him. I yearned to take him into my arms and comfort him. But I realized that even such an innocent gesture might easily be misconstrued, so I restrained myself.

When we entered the woods, I rested against the lichen-covered trunk on ancient oak tree, fiddling with a twig, my mind full of strategies to try to reassure him and keep him here at Escape.

Jimmy stuck a grass stem between his full, wine-colored lips. "I realize no relationship with you is possible. The most I can hope for is a deep and cherished friendship."

He reached his hand toward the trunk next to me to support himself. I pressed my back against the bark.

"I hope you won't take this the wrong way, but I have to confess that since we first spoke at the county jail, I have grown to care very deeply for you." He removed the grass blade from his mouth and leaned in close to me, his cheek nearly grazing mine. I felt my resistance melting, and touched a branch to steady myself.

"Uh," I said, "I—"

"Shh," he whispered, and put his finger across my lips. "You don't have to answer me. I don't expect you to reciprocate my feelings." He ran his hand through my hair and caressed my cheek. Then, with his fingertips, he traced the nape of my neck. A rush of searing tingles raced along my spine.

I started to tremble, and looked down. He lifted my chin and looked at me. I lost myself for a moment in his slate-blue eyes. He smiled so invitingly, and I gazed at him with incredible desire. He moved ever so gradually closer, bringing his lips close to mine, when suddenly I bolted.

"What?" he called. "Wait! Where are you going?"

I stopped a few yards away, gasping at my close escape. I knew I should keep on running and never look back, but I turned and said, "I know what you're up to, and it's never going to work!"

"Paul, come back. I was only offering my devoted friendship," he said. "Like brothers. I know I would have to earn your respect."

"It's against Scripture!" I yelled. "It's not what's best for you!" I felt confused and embarrassed and so full of yearning I could only mutter platitudes from Ruth.

"But I only want what's best for you!" he cried.

Sly's words rang in my ears, "Get thee behind me, Satan," but I knew he would only laugh at me. "You'd better leave."

"Why must I leave? Didn't you want me to come visit you? Isn't that why you came to see me, cultivated my friendship?"

"You—you're putting my recovery in jeopardy."

"Paul, come back. That's the last thing I would want. Your faith is an inspiration to me!"

I stopped, suddenly ashamed at my own selfishness. Here he was, earnestly reaching out to me for support, and I was about to spurn him because of my own weak will. What happened to my noble effort to convert him and bring him into the fold? Yet I knew if I delayed a moment longer, a fall would take place.

"Go away!" I shouted, and ran all the way back to the ranch.

18: Precious Bodily Fluids

While Sly was preoccupied with his latest project, Jackson took over the water filter sales in our campus outlet. The office was open for a few hours each afternoon, mostly selling to tourists who passed through the wooded reserves surrounding the lakes of Chagrin's water district. They'd notice our sign by the side of the road: "Crystal Spring Water Filters—For Your Precious Bodily Fluids!"

On weekends, Jackson had Perry and Sheila out working the street fairs. It was a no-risk opportunity for all of us to get involved in the business without being entirely dependent on our success. Jackson already had dollar signs in his eyes, anticipating the time when he would be able to go off on his own and reap the benefits of his pyramid-building schemes, rather than having all the profits absorbed by Escape.

Under a banner that said, "Let's Rap About Water," Jackson set up a table at one of the many street fairs that take place in Chagrin County during the summer and fall. This one was held in the town square in Mill Valley, which was soon filled with throngs of people throughout the Bay Area looking for an escape from the summer fog. Booths hawked everything from leather goods to tie-dyed T-shirts, ceramics, soft sculptures and stuffed animals, all made by local artisans. Mixed among the crafts were numerous animal groups, like Save the Whales, Stop Animal Testing, and Gorilla Rights Now; environmentalists, like Save the Wetlands, Save the Redwoods, and Save the River. Then there were community groups, supporting health plans, after-school activities, and school bonds.

After taking my stint at the table, I wandered among the booths until I came across this one advertising help for young gay people: "Teen Spirit," it was called, part of Rainbow Life, a ministry to the gay community. I went up to their table and told them I was also part of an outreach team for young gays. "We help young homosexuals like myself get off the street and out of the lifestyle," I said.

The woman at the booth was middle-aged, had soft brown hair with streaks of gray. She looked at me quizzically through her glasses. "'Out of the lifestyle'?"

"Sure," I said. "It's called 'Escape,' and we offer young gays an alternative to a life of sin and degradation."

"I'm not sure that you understand our mission," she said. "We help young gays feel okay about being gay."

"You what?" I said.

"We don't think there's anything wrong with being gay."

"And you call yourselves a church?"

"Yes, we do. Jesus never said anything against homosexuality, and he taught us to love our neighbors as ourselves. Maybe you'd like to come to one of our meetings?" She held out a brochure.

I hesitated for a moment, curious about the Scriptural distortions she was no doubt offering unsuspecting gays, but after my encounter with Jimmy I decided it was best not to submit myself to any further distractions. "I don't think so," I said.

"Well, we meet every Thursday night if you ever change your mind."

I stepped away from her, and then saw the booth right next to hers was recruiting gays to come live in their neighborhood! It was called Redwood Glen. They even had a newspaper article announcing their plan to invite gays to live among them. "Gays Make Good Neighbors," ran the headline. A spokesperson said, "They keep up property values, care about diversity, and get involved with their community."

I thought, what is this world coming to? Now we even have church groups that have totally succumbed to homosexual propaganda. There is so little understanding for what Escape is trying to accomplish.

I got back to our booth, where Jackson was deeply engrossed in closing a sale with a customer. "If you sign up today, you get an introductory sales kit for only $599.95, plus a discount on your own filter. You get in on the ground floor of this exciting opportunity, plus you get all the tax breaks that come along with owning your own business. It's the American way!"

Sheila, meanwhile, was pouring pond water through the filter. Then, with a flourish, she offered the glass of crystal clear water to Perry, who took it with some trepidation, and gulped it down.

The customer left with all these forms and boxes. Jackson stuck the credit slip in his sales book, and then started his spiel: "Step right up, try the fresh-tasting water from Crystal Springs Water Filters, revive your precious bodily fluids with pure, healthy water free of pesticides, fungicides, organic poisons, lead and fluoride…"

Perry told Sheila he'd been drinking so much water he had to go pee. After he left, Sheila whispered to me, "Let's get out of here."

"I just took a break."

"Jackson is so into it he won't even notice. Besides, I saw this booth I want to show you."

We walked past various stalls until we came to an area that wasn't laid out in neat rows like the rest of the fair, but snaked around in a spiral. Overhead was a banner that proclaimed, "Welcome to the Psychic Faire!" Then below was a smaller sign that said, "Today at the Tarot Booth—Madame Blavatsky Reveals Your Fortune."

I stopped at the gate. "Do you really think we should go in there?"

"Of course, this should be a scream."

"But Sly said, 'Do not turn to mediums or wizards.'"

"Come on, it's not going to kill you." She took me by the hand and pulled me trough the gate. I gave up my resistance and followed along. We wound our way through a maze of booths hawking various psychic wares and services: crystals and worry beads, Bach flowers and aroma therapy, past lives and aura cleansing. The smoky smell of musk incense mixed with jasmine and patchouli. The sound of tabla drums thumped in the background, and a sitar pierced the chatter of the crowds with its ethereal wail. We overheard snippets of conversations from the people around us:

One woman in a tie-dyed pants suit said, "I had a dialogue with my Spirit Guide."

Her companion, wearing a paisley caftan, said "Oh? What did she tell you?"

"She said that all was well, and I was on the brink of abundance."

"Well I discovered that in a past life, I was Marie Antoinette."

"Ooh, that is such heavy Karma. You'll have to work really hard to make up for that one."

I leaned over to Sheila. "Yes, I think it's been about fifteen lives so far, but up to now I've managed to have my cake, and eat it too!"

"You are such a cynic."

"Really, though, isn't it interesting that practically no one ever realizes in a former life they were Jake the plumber on the lower east side. They were always Napoleon, or Nijinsky, or Cleopatra."

We came to a booth that advertised an Astral Travel Agency: "Take a Dream Flight to the World's Power Spots! Fire Walk in Machu Picchu, Dance with Shadow Puppets in Bali, Commune with the Druids at Stonehenge!"

Sheila looked at the brochure. "Ooh, pricy!" she exclaimed. "I never knew traveling on the Astral Plane could be so expensive!"

"I have a confession to make. The other night, I channeled Barbie."

"The doll?"

"Yes! It's hard to believe, but with so many girls aspiring to be like her, she has actually materialized on the spirit channel."

"The 'spirit channel?'" she said, raising her brow.

"Next to the weather channel."

She elbowed me in the ribs. We passed a couple of other booths, one with a sign that asked, "Are You an Angel?" Its walls were covered with lovely portraits of famous angels, like Michael and Gabriel. The next one proclaimed, "Ghosts Are Real!" with numerous testimonials about mysterious noises and documented sightings, with a Psychic Faire Special on the "Spook Rebuke," which contained secret methods for appeasing apparitions. Then there was Dialogue With Your Dog, or how to communicate with your pet using mental telepathy.

My favorite display was the booth on Alien Abductions. According to recent surveys, one out of forty Americans has reported contact with aliens. Respected scientists have interviewed dozens of abductees who exhibit no observable signs of mental illness. The stories show an incredible consistency: tested and often sexually probed by aliens who look remarkably similar to ET, abductees then return to earth, often with unusual psychic powers. We are being prepared for an invasion that will either save us, or enslave us.

Suddenly, we heard the hollow sound of a Tibetan gong. We turned around, and faced a booth that was draped with silk scarves. "Oh, this is it!" Sheila said.

In the midst of a Persian carpet, piled all around with fringed satin pillows, sat an older woman wearing a turban. She wore hoop earrings and a necklace of bronze coins. A broach with a tear-shaped amethyst clung to her dress, which was made of purple velvet with strips of brocade decorated by signs of the Zodiac. On a small table was a deck of cards. A notice announced psychic readings from the Tarot.

"Oh, no way," I said.

"If you don't believe in any of this stuff, it's hardly going to warp your mind," Sheila said.

I still pulled back.

She stepped right up to the medium and said, "I'd like a reading for my friend," and paid her.

I decided what the hell. It's just a parlor game, like the Ouija Board. My mom used to throw the I Ching all the time when I was a kid, and nothing bad ever happened. I said, "Hi," and sat down on the carpet next to her.

The Reader gave me a long look, sizing me up, but I tried not to give her any clues. "My name is Madame Blavatsky," she said in this totally bogus Transylvanian accent. She sounded like some low-budget Dracula movie from the 'forties. "I can tell you are a nullifidian." I looked at her, not quite getting it. "A skeptic," she explained, "but no matter. There is no need for beliefs in wizardry. I myself make no claims to supernatural powers. It is all," she said, with a flourish of her hand, "in the cards."

19: Walking Along the Precipice

She shuffled the cards and asked me to split the deck. Then she placed ten cards face up on the carpet, with four cards surrounding two cards crossed in the middle, and four along the side.

"Ah," she said, taking in the pattern as a whole. "Now I'm beginning to see. A very comprehensive picture."

Yeah right, I thought. Then she started in and I must admit, though I was skeptical at first, she definitely read my beads.

She pointed to the card in the center of the square. "The first card represents your current situation."

The card showed a chariot drawn by two sphinxes, one black, and one white. A canopy hung behind the bare-chested charioteer, who carried a scepter. "What does it mean?"

"The Chariot symbolizes the problems that can be overcome when true effort is brought into harmony with a clear direction," she explained. "The quality it represents is perseverance in the face of adversity." She looked at me to gauge my response.

Outwardly, I tried to remain calm, but my mind was already churning. After my recent encounter with Jimmy, I wasn't that certain I could persevere in much of anything.

"I see conflicting influences," she continued, "and the need for supervision. There is an urgency to gain control of one's emotions. This card suggests that you can achieve your goal when you reach a balance between your physical and mental powers."

I could see clearly that Sly and Jimmy represented my conflicting influences—Sly was obviously my supervisor. And boy, did I ever feel conflicted!

"The second card crosses the first, and relates to your immediate future."

This card showed a man with an infinity sign hovering over his head. In his left hand he held a rod pointing upward, his other hand pointing down.

"This is the Magician," she explained, "with one hand pointing toward heaven, the other toward the earth. That means heavenly influence can be used on earth by those who are aware of its divine power. This card suggests creativity and self-reliance, but is tinged with an aspect of guile, deception, and trickery."

Trickery, that's for sure. The devil's a wily seducer. By this time, I was anxious for her to go on.

She pointed to the card above the first two. "The third card is your goal, or destiny. It indicates the best possible outcome."

A flaming cherub appeared in the sky above a man and a woman, both naked. Nearby, a tree entwined by a serpent bore various fruits.

"The Lovers card represents an unexpected event or meeting. It symbolizes love, of course, and the beginning of romance—also, letting oneself go. It partakes of the struggle between the sacred and the profane, and suggests temptation, or possible predicaments. The other interesting aspect is that this is the sixth card of the Major Arcana, in the third step. Six is twice thrice, so finding the Lovers in this position doubles its significance. Love, even profane love, will be hard to resist."

So that was it: Jimmy no doubt represented my profane temptation and current predicament. I would have to work doubly hard to persevere in my quest for true salvation.

Next, she pointed to the card on the right. "The fourth card exemplifies the influences of the past, which are now embodied in the Questioner."

This card showed a skeleton riding a horse, mowing down people with a scythe, heads and hands and even his own foot flying through the air. I must have looked worried.

"Never fear. The Death card indicates transformation. It can mean loss or failure, but it can also mean an abrupt change of the old self, being born anew. Facing to the right suggests looking toward the future and possible talents that are still unfulfilled."

Ah, this card obviously shows how I've died to my old sinful self, and am born anew in Christ. But I haven't yet fulfilled my promise.

She indicated the card below. "The fifth card is the recent past, revealing the events that influence your current state."

This card showed a man hanging upside down, tied by his left ankle to a horizontal beam supported by two bare tree trunks. He bent his right leg at the knee, forming a triangle, his hands tied behind his back.

"The Hanged Man shows life in suspension. It suggests a reversal of the mind and one's way of life. It recalls events of an uncertain nature; repentance; and the need for readjustment. I also see the aspect of an unappreciated person."

Well, I certainly reversed my way of life, and it's sure taking some readjustment. I wondered who I'm not appreciating? No doubt, I should stop making fun of Ruth.

"The sixth card represents future influence." She pointed to the card on the far left. I shuddered. It showed a grotesque creature with bat-like wings and the horns of a ram, a woman's breasts, and the legs of a goat.

"The Devil represents bad advice and misguided dependence on another person. I see controversy, shock, and temptation toward evil—and the seeming inability to realize one's goals."

This was really depressing. I felt alarmed at the warning that despite my best efforts, I may never reach my goal. It only goes to confirm that I can't count on Jimmy, who would no doubt lead me down a path of temptation and sin.

She pointed to the bottom card on the right row. "The seventh card represents you, the Questioner, in your current position, with all the influences that surround you."

A young man, blindfolded and wearing a foolscap, walked along a precipice, carrying a bundle at the end of his staff, a dog nipping at his heel.

Madame Blavatsky smiled. "The Fool represents the beginning of an adventure, with enthusiasm and passion. Unfortunately, there's a tendency to embark on a project without carefully considering all the ramifications, and a reluctance to listen to the advice of others. Walking along the precipice suggests an inattentiveness to important details, rashness and folly, a lack of discipline, even delirium. I see an element of infatuation—" here she leaned close to me—"perhaps an indiscretion."

I blushed. Talk about walking along the precipice! I felt like I was about to be catapulted into the abyss.

"The eighth card looks at your social context—your influence on others, as well as their effect on you."

This card showed a dog and a wolf baying at the Moon as it rose between two towers. In the foreground, a large red crayfish crawled out of the water.

"The Moon represents the Night—deception, trickery, and disillusionment. It's a sign of caution against insincerity. The crayfish suggests ulterior motives, often of a sexual nature. I see the coming together of many divergent influences. You may be taken advantage of by an insincere relationship."

Whoa! I'd have to be on my guard!

"The ninth card represents inner emotions—your own turmoil and secret desires."

I steeled myself for this one. It showed a narrow stone tower with three windows, the turret struck by a bolt of lightning hurtling out of the sun. Two people fell out of the tower, including one wearing a crown.

"The Falling Tower represents the breakdown of old beliefs and changing values. It suggests the abandoning of a past relationship or severing a friendship. How the mighty shall fall! I see ruin, moral bankruptcy—a sudden event that destroys trust."

I squirmed at this sign of betrayal, wondering how it related to my own secret desires.

"The tenth and last card, interestingly enough, is also the tenth card of the Major Arcana: the Wheel of Fortune. This card represents the final result, the culmination of all the influences revealed so far."

Seated on top of a large wheel was a Sphinx holding a sword; to its left side was a snake, on its right a figure with a deer-like face. Strange signs and figures marked the eight spokes of the wheel.

"The Wheel of Fortune represents special gain, or unusual loss. In the culmination of your question, unexpected events may occur, implying good or bad luck, depending on the influence of the other aspects." She paused here a moment to survey the entire spread. "There is definitely an element of change in the air. With perseverance, you may be able to master this change."

Did this mean I would succeed in my goal of freeing myself from this awful demon?

She soon dashed my optimism. "Your naivete suggests, however, that you are subject to deception and bad influences."

"Is there any way I can counter these influences?"

"I would say, trust your basic instincts, your intuition, your most heartfelt desires. Be cautious, however, about plunging headlong into rash decisions, which may lead to folly."

I thought, oh that helps a lot. What a windbag. I thanked her and we got up to leave. Sheila took my arm as we walked through the stalls. "Wasn't that terrific?" she asked.

I had to admit I was impressed at first. "But towards the end, I don't know. It seemed like she just says whatever you want to hear."

"But how do you suppose she knows what that is?"

I dismissed her question with a wave of my hand. "It could be this way or that way, depending. Depending on what?"

"Well," said Sheila, "depending on what you put into it."

There's the rub.

20: Cyberspace Cadet

When we got back to the ranch, I discovered that instead of leaving, Jimmy had apologized to Sly and actually joined up with Escape! Sly believed him, I suppose, because he fits perfectly into his notion about Saul of Tarsus. Jimmy has supposedly finally come around, humble and penitent, and settled into our routine.

This made me awfully nervous, and at first I avoided him. Remembering my Tarot, I wondered what it meant that he was going to be a continuing influence. Secretly I was glad he came back—my heart lifted when Sly told me—perhaps I hadn't let something important slip away, after all. Yet I felt a strange foreboding. I couldn't say anything about it to Sly, of course; he would be furious that Jimmy had tried to seduce me. Although I felt vulnerable being around him, somehow I couldn't bear the thought of Sly sending him away. I would simply have to trust my instincts and try to persevere, like Madame Blavatsky said.

Realizing I was ripe for temptation and unsavory influences, I went looking for Sly to see if his new treatment was anywhere near ready, 'cause I could really use it. I found him in his office, with his feet on the desk, relaxing for the first time in weeks.

"All of this," he said, taking in the room with a wave of his hand, "is nostalgia." He batted the bomber, Enola Gay, and it rotated at the end of its wire. "You can't make a living by living in the past! Nor by rescuing wayward waifs like yourself. Oh sure, we get a few centavos at garage sales, some guilt money from my videos of gay parades, but that doesn't cut it. Even our water filter sales haven't kept up with our expenses."

Then he told me about his computer project. "The future," he declared, "lies in Virtual Reality." He motioned for me to follow him. We went down the hall and he unlocked a door next to the treatment room. On the door was a tiny plaque, which read: "Welcome to the Magic Theater—Price of Admission—Your Mind." I recognized this phrase from Hesse's *Steppenwolf*, which I read in high school while stoned. It gave me an eerie feeling.

Sly swung open the door, revealing a stark, windowless room set up with a bank of computers along one wall, and a strange-looking vehicle supported by pneumatic pistons. "Welcome to Cyberspace."

He explained that his Virtual Reality machine embodies the essence of the multi-modal approach—it combines sensory input with mind, body, and imagery in a live presentational environment.

"Put on your Cyberware, then you can board the inner space ship." Sly handed me a suit of tight-fitting overalls. "This is your body glove," he explained, "with sensory inputs throughout the suit."

I stripped down to my shorts and pulled on the lycra suit. I could see my reflection in one of the computer monitors. With metallic racing stripes and bolts of lightning on my shoulders, I looked vaguely like a skinny superhero.

I crawled into the contraption, which resembled those rockets they had outside of supermarkets when I was a kid. It included headphones inside a display helmet, suspended from above so you don't feel any weight, a glove input for my right hand, and a joy stick for the left. Down at my feet was a brake and an accelerator. Sly explained that besides the joy stick, I could also influence the ship's direction by leaning forward, backward, or from side to side.

"You've got your hypermedia all in one comprehensive cyberworld package—your stereo sound, images and text formatted with interactive capabilities—musical score, animation, full-color graphics and feature-length video. Stick your head inside that brain bucket."

I put my face up against the display unit and Sly flicked on a switch. I suddenly found myself flying through the Grand Canyon.

"Actually, these 3-D graphics are far better refined than what you usually think of as computer imaging. I've souped up my computers to warp speed—imaging at thirty frames per second, just like a movie, instead of the old ten. It's no longer cartoon figures, but photo-realism. Grab your joy stick and take it for a whirl."

I leaned forward and headed upriver, passing eroded cliffs of orange and scarlet sandstone, hovering over mesas a thousand feet from the canyon floor, then zooming between pinnacles and pulling up at the last minute, surprising a bald eagle off its rook.

When I pulled on the stick, the rocket tilted backwards and pressed against me as I catapulted up and up, over the desert, high into the stratosphere until I could see the whole of the western states, the outline of California against the blue Pacific, the rim of the Earth's atmosphere like a thin halo encircling the globe.

"From your glove inputs you can access portals into other worlds," he said.

I reached out my hand toward the moon, and turned it around. Like entering a black hole, I was pulled toward outer space and found myself circling Jupiter, right above its red spot. I'd always been curious about this mysterious patch, so I zoomed in for a closer look. I found a myself buffeted by a swirling red hurricane as big as North America, the smell of ammonia so strong it nearly gagged me. I veered away, and headed across Saturn's rings, through an obstacle course of asteroids, past the dry deserts of Mars, and finally back to planet Earth. A shower of meteorites came hurtling by just as I re-entered the atmosphere, and they blazed in glory like a fireworks display off my starboard bow. I took one more trip around the globe, then zeroed in on San Francisco Bay for a landing. I felt a little queasy, but it was quite a thrill, kind of like a cyber-age roller coaster.

"My laser scan can duplicate your three-dimensional body and incorporate it into any image onscreen."

Hearing Sly's voice after this awesome voyage was a little disorienting. "What?" I said, and removed my head from the visor.

"Step over here." I got out of the ship, and Sly had me stand on a rotating platform in front of this device which looked like an X-ray machine. It cast a red, vertical beam along the full length of my body as I turned around. Then Sly took a CD from the machine and inserted it into a CD player in the bank of computers.

"Look in the visor," Sly said.

I peaked inside and a hologram of myself sprang to life before my very eyes.

"Use your glove to move him about."

I reached out to touch him (or me; I was getting a little confused), and saw myself rotate around, move my arms, walk, squat, jump and run far away until I nearly disappeared, and then come back, very close, until I was looking right into my eyes.

"Go further," Sly suggested.

"I'm right up against my face."

"Just keep going," he said.

I went past my face and into my mind. Suddenly, a whole other world opened up. I could see myself lying on my bed in the bunkhouse, walking around the ranch, and sitting in Bible class. Then I saw myself having dinner with my mother! And even heard a conversation I had long ago forgotten: "What do you want to do after you graduate?" she asked. At the time I was still in high school.

"I don't know," I said. "I'll sing in a rock band, and do a concert tour for world peace."

"You don't even play an instrument. Why don't you find something a little more down to earth?"

"Singers don't have to play any instruments."

"Well that's true," she said. And then she surprised me, given all her Janice Joplin albums: "Nowadays, they don't even have to know how to sing."

I was embarrassed, and hoped Sly couldn't overhear any of this. Seeing images in my own mind come to life was too weird, so I stepped back out of my brain and pulled away from the helmet.

I turned to the Rev and said, "So this is what you've been working on all this time."

He smiled and puffed out his chest, obviously proud of himself.

The next question I was almost afraid to ask, but I knew I needed something, and hoped Virtual Reality might just do the trick. "So how does this fit into our treatment?"

"I'm glad you asked." Sly rubbed the hood of the vehicle. "This little baby creates a Virtual World. It can transport you at warp speed to the farthest reaches of your imagination. It can be used for idle entertainment, or to confront your inner demons." He went on to explain that hyper-fiction offers multiple routes through a story. "This program resembles our previous experiments: you can go with the naked guys, or you can make love to a woman."

I must have recoiled a bit, remembering the electric shocks from the earlier treatment.

"Don't worry, no jolts to the pecker this time," he assured me in his usual crude way. "Your reinforcement comes from the experience itself. You have your free will to choose heaven or hell, depending on which way you decide to go—rather like life, if you think about it."

"Well, here goes nothing," I said, and climbed into the cockpit.

"Correction," Sly said. "Here goes everything that you've been working up to until this very moment!" He paused, as if he thought better of this. "Not to put any pressure on you."

I put my face up to the visor and inserted my hand into the sensory-input glove.

"All systems check!" Sly said. I held up my thumb. He threw the switch and I heard the high-pitched hum of the computers whir into gear. I grasped hold of the joy stick and braced myself for my healing voyage into Cyberspace.

21: Into the Vortex

I was immediately plunged into a virtual world of sensual sights, sounds, and smells: it resembled a Roman orgy, with dozens of exquisitely-built men in loose, revealing togas lounging about on pillows feasting on a lavish buffet: suckling pigs revolved on rotisseries and sides of beef stewed in their own juices. Troops of slave boys arrived with platters of turkeys, legs of lamb, roast potatoes, carrots, and yams. Young men lounged about, licking the grease from their lips, their fingers, and off each other's nipples!

A huge fire roared in the hearth, and torches stuck in the arched columns cast a warm glow over the sumptuous repast. Slave boys played the lyre or dangled bunches of grapes over the gaping mouths of the participants. A chorus line of young men pranced before the fire, their shadows leaping on the stone ramparts.

Like the proverbial fly on the wall, I could navigate among the participants at will, taking in any view I wanted, watching every move, exploring every crevice. I zoomed in close to a couple of youths who were kissing in the shadows, gradually unloosing their togas, which fell in a heap around them as they stroked each other's chests and thighs, pressing their hips together in a sensuous embrace.

I felt like the ultimate voyeur, as I could not only watch but with my sensory input glove could also touch and stroke and participate in the orgy of grappling bodies that surrounded me, to the point where I lost myself in homoerotic delights, and completely forgot my task in coming here.

I joined the pair making love in the shadows, intertwining my limbs with theirs. Gradually, the blond youth slipped away and left me with the darker fellow, whose iridescent teeth gleamed in the firelight when he threw back his head, laughing in ecstasy as I thrust myself upon him. He looked at me knowingly, and I discovered it was Jimmy!

I tried to pull away, but he grasped me tighter, pulling me closer. In a flash I questioned how Sly had managed to scan Jimmy's naked body into the computer, but this did not distract me long before I plunged into our passionate embrace. He thrust his hips against me and I entered him completely, ready to explode! Then the most peculiar sensation flooded through me as I continued to be drawn into his body—my hips and legs, my torso and arms, my head and shoulders were all sucked towards him! The electric feeling that had pulsed through my genitals now extended throughout my body as I plunged deep inside him.

Before long, the pleasant sensations left me as it became dark and steamy, with fetid odors and grotesque lumps of waste, fungus, and bacterial colonies greasing my journey with slime, until I reached a second portal, which had a sign posted at the entrance, lit by a smoky, flickering torch: Abandon All Hope, Ye Who Enter Here.

With another spasm, I was thrust through the sphincter into the next level of Hell. I smelled the stench of sulfur, could make out bubbling cauldrons of mud, then I slipped into a scorching river of magma, which rushed into a surge of rapids plunging through the canyon walls.

Howling along the banks of this raging torrent I caught glimpses of Leonardo da Vinci, an arrow piercing his side, his face plastered with a mysterious, Giaconda smile; Michelangelo, his hand stretching vainly into the void towards a God that had forsaken him; Oscar Wilde, his youthful portrait beside his own face, grown haggard; Walt Whitman, his sinewy arms clinging to a young man as they both sank howling into the magma. These scenes were followed by lesser-known inverts—some crucified, others roasting over fiery pits or clamped in stocks and pinned by thumbscrews, all gnashing their teeth in eternal anguish.

Then I heard, as if from a voice of thunder, "Come!" and I veered toward the mouth of the canyon.

And behold, a pale horse, its rider's name was Death, and Hades followed him—they were given power over a fourth of the earth, to kill with sword and famine, pestilence and by wild beasts.

Then there was a great earthquake, and the sun became black as sackcloth, the moon became like blood, and the stars of the sky fell to the earth as the fig tree sheds its winter fruit when shaken by a gale; the sky vanished like a scroll that is rolled up, and every mountain and island was removed from its place.

Then the smoke from the shaft of a bottomless pit rose like the smoke of a great furnace, and the sun and the air were darkened. From the smoke came locusts on the earth, and they were given power like the sting of scorpions. They were allowed to torture those who have not the seal of God upon their foreheads, but not to kill them. These wretched souls sought death, but could not find it: they longed to die, yet death flew from them.

Then I heard a voice again say, "The beast that ascends from the bottomless pit will make war upon them and conquer them and kill them, and their dead bodies will lie in the street of the great city which is called Sodom."

And another portent appeared in heaven: behold a great red Dragon, with seven heads and ten horns, and seven diadems upon his heads. His tail swept down a third of the stars of heaven, and cast them to the earth.

And I saw a beast rising out of the sea, with ten horns and seven heads, with ten diadems upon its horns and a blasphemous name upon its heads. And the beast that I saw was like a leopard, its feet were like a bear's and its mouth was like a lion's mouth. And to it the dragon gave his power and his throne and great authority.

Then the great voice (which sounded strangely like Sly) continued: "If any one worships the beast and its image, and receives a mark on his forehead or on his hand, he also shall drink the wine of God's wrath, poured unmixed into the cup of his anger, and he shall be tormented with fire and brimstone in the presence of the holy angels and in the presence of the Lamb."

Then an angel poured his bowl on the sun, and it was allowed to scorch men with fire; men were scorched by the fierce heat, and they cursed the name of God who had power over these plagues, and they did not repent and give Him glory.

Then once again, the voice called out: "I am the Alpha and the Omega, the beginning and the end. To the thirsty I will give water without price from the fountain of the water of life. But as for the cowardly, the faithless, the polluted, as for murderers, fornicators, sorcerers, idolaters, and all liars, their lot shall be in the lake that burns with fire and brimstone, which is the second death.

"He who has an ear, let him hear! Behold, I stand at the door and knock; if anyone hears my voice and opens the door, I will come in to him and eat with him, and he with me."

And as the fires from the torrent of magma rose around me, the howls of the wretched, tortured souls filled the smoky air, I suddenly remembered that I did not have to stay in this fiery pit, caught in a whirlpool of passionate abominations: He is standing at the door, all I have to do is open the portal to another world, and I shall be released.

22: Amazing Grace

I looked up toward the sky to find the moon, it's face obscured by the dark smoke. Grasping my joy stick, I leaned back and accelerated into the sky. I touched the moon, which sighed with a celestial voice, and turned inside out. I found myself in another world: a heavenly place, with soft clouds and angels playing lilting tunes on harps and lyres. Lying on a bed of clouds, I discovered a voluptuous woman lounging against satin pillows, her face veiled, beckoning to me with her long, bejeweled fingers.

At first I was suspicious—was this image another enticing Jezebel, tempting me to fornication? Or was she my ticket to liberation from unnatural lust?

I gulped hard, and climbed onto her bed. She took me into her arms and caressed me. Her skin was soft and pliant, her hair silky. She felt so different from the tough muscles, acrid smells and salty taste of hot, sweating men. Yet she smelled so strongly of rose blossoms, I sneezed. But instead of taking offense, she laughed and blessed me. She gradually brought me forth, penetrating her many folds until I reached her warm interior wetness.

Caressing me as I lay cradled in her breasts, she began to work her magic down below until I expanded and filled her inner world. Then once again, I felt this peculiar sensation as the rest of my body was slowly sucked inside her. She lifted her veil to kiss my forehead as I disappeared, revealing her face for the first time. As I raised my eyes to gaze upon her, I was shocked to see it was Ruth!

I struggled to break free of her tight grip, but it was too late. I was swallowed up by her many folds, and found myself on a journey down yet another canal. I slid along easily enough through the smooth channel, until I came to a skin sheath that blocked any further penetration. I could not back up, nor in any way get around it.

When I touched it, it talked to me—"So wide, can't get around it, so low, can't get under it, so high, can't get over it—oh bless my soul. You're just gonna have to push through it, honey."

I was pressed up against the wall with a mighty force until finally, in a thrust of crimson and a burst of milky white fluid, I spurted through it. At this point, my body became like a tadpole with a terrific tail that propelled me forward as I swam in a current against a tide of fluids which rushed past me, competing with other tadpoles that shoved and battered me against the sides of the canal. We jumped and thrashed like salmon leaping upstream. I finally reached another threshold shaped like a donut, it's center a closed sphincter that I tried to approach along with the hordes of other tadpoles, pushing and shoving each other out of the way. I wriggled and squirmed to the front until finally I got my nose into the button and plunged through.

I found myself in a strange and watery world: a calm pool compared to the wild torrent I'd left behind. I turned somersaults and loop-de-loops and spun in delight in my new-found freedom. But soon I noticed, one by one, other tadpoles making it through the sphincter, and streaming ahead of me. I knew that there was one mad rush left—I wasn't sure towards what fate, but felt certain my ultimate goal still lay before me. I pressed onward.

When floating in the middle of the pool, bathed in radiant light, we came upon a giant, luminous egg. Tadpoles had gathered at its edges, butting their blind heads against it, but none could penetrate its thick membrane. I scurried this way and that, looking for an opening, but there was none to be found.

Undaunted, I knew that uniting with this egg was my destiny, so I backed up and lunged toward its surface with a mighty thump, and was nearly knocked cold for my trouble. I swam around and around, crowding out other tadpoles from likely looking spots, then scanning again. Finally, I let go of all my rational strategies, and simply willed myself to join with her. Wriggling with all my force against the barrier, suddenly I was in. A protective shell formed around us. We opened our nuclei, and mixed our genes. There was no more us, but only I, a New Being.

Once realizing she had been taken, the other tadpoles soon tired and fell away. Multiplying our cells, we attached ourselves with a lifeline to the wall of the cavern, from which we received nourishment from our host. The music of the spheres played gently in the background, sounding surprisingly like "Amazing Grace."

Suspended in the precious amniotic fluid, I floated in a watery world, the heartbeat above me in synch with my own.

23: Face to Face

After my treatment with the Virtual Reality machine, I became calmer and more secure in my salvation. Something seemed to snap into place, like the missing piece of a puzzle, and suddenly I was restored to my natural condition. Not that anyone should ever become cocky or complacent about homosexual recovery, but I felt substantial relief from my previous urges, and less tempted to return to my old ways.

I was even able to stand being around Jimmy, who also seemed more subdued in his participation in our life together. Having grown up in the church, like Perry, he was familiar with many stories from the Bible. His faith, though it had lapsed, was now all the stronger from having overcome the devil's influence. Sly explained that Jimmy's experience with degradation and redemption had probably inoculated him against any further temptation. "Trust in him, who speaketh from the heart, for there lieth the truth," Sly assured me.

Over the weeks, Jimmy taught me to appreciate our Bible lessons with Ruth, which before he came I had merely tolerated. In contrast to all the hellfire and brimstone, he showed me the Beatitudes, where the meek shall inherit the Kingdom of Heaven; and Ecclesiastes:

> For everything, there is a season
> and a time for every matter under heaven:
> A time to be born, and a time to die;
> A time to sow, and a time to reap—

I'd always thought this was a rock song by the Byrds, when all along it was from the Bible! And he introduced me to the Song of Solomon, with its lovely poetry:

> As an apple tree among the trees of the wood,
> So is my beloved among young men.
> With great delight I sat in his shadow,
> and his fruit was sweet to my taste.
> He brought me to the banqueting house,
> and his banner over me was love.
> Sustain me with raisins, refresh me with apples;
> for I am sick with love.
> O that his left hand were under my head,
> and that his right hand embraced me!

It made me eager to discover other gems secreted away amongst all the dreary condemnations, plagues, and genealogies. Meanwhile, the Rev was prepping us for our debut at the annual Convention for Ex-Gay Ministries, sponsored by RELEASE—Religious Ex-gays Living Evangelically Against Sin and Ecumenicism.

This year's theme was "Reclaiming America," and was being held in Anaheim. Sly wanted us to be the featured speakers during his workshop on Virtual Reality. All we had to do was testify how we had once fallen into the homosexual lifestyle, and then through the grace of Our Lord (and the help of Sly's new treatment), had healed our sexual brokenness and were now living a New Life in the Resurrection.

Sly said Virtual Reality was considered very controversial. There were factions on the conference planning committee who had spoken out against it (they felt it was too graphic—even pornographic), but in the end Sly prevailed. He said testimonials would confirm and validate the efficacy of his new treatment modality.

Then the next day he'd take us all to Disneyland! Sly wanted Jimmy and me to become a team—he could see us witnessing and lecturing together, recruiting others, and visiting other towns. He said after our debut at the convention, our options would be wide open. He had no doubt he could book us to speak with him at a huge rally against special rights for homosexuals.

* * *

The night before we left for the conference, Jimmy showed me First Corinthians 13, the love chapter. We were in our bunks, and Jimmy had been reading for a while. Jackson and Perry were already fast asleep. I was lying on my back, my hands behind my head, smelling the musty smells of the pine cabin. I felt content, yet excited about our debut at the conference the next day.

"Listen to this," Jimmy whispered. He sat up and swung his legs over the side of the bed. He was wearing shorts and a T-shirt, and light from the kerosene lantern highlighted the dark hairs on his forearms and thighs. He leaned his elbows on his knees, holding the Bible in the light of the flickering lamp. "'If I speak in the tongues of men and of angels, but have not love, I am a noisy gong or a clanging cymbal.'"

I turned on my side and leaned on my elbow, listening to him read.

"'And if I have prophetic powers, and understand all mysteries and all knowledge, and if I have all faith, so as to remove mountains, but have not love, I am nothing.'" he read. "Then it says, 'If I give away all I have, and if I deliver my body to be burned, but have not love, I gain nothing.'"

He looked up from the text. "Isn't that something?" Then he recited the next part while looking in my eyes. "'Love is patient and kind, love is not jealous or boastful, it is not arrogant or rude. Love does not insist on its own way; it is not irritable or resentful; it does not rejoice at wrong, but rejoices in the right. Love bears all things, believes all things, hopes all things, endures all things.'"

I found myself gazing at him, almost transfixed. "That's lovely," I said.

"'Love never ends,'" he read again. I liked watching his lips move, his Adam's apple bob up and down. His sonorous voice vibrated through the hard metal frame of my bunk. "'As for prophecy, it will pass away; as for tongues, they will cease; as for knowledge, it will pass away. For our knowledge is imperfect and our prophecy is imperfect; but when the perfect comes, the imperfect will pass away.'"

How do we know when the perfect comes, I wondered. Then I remembered Madam Blavatsky: trust your intuition.

"'When I was a child, I spoke like a child, I thought like a child, I reasoned like a child; when I became a man, I gave up childish ways. For now we see in a mirror dimly, but then face to face.'" Jimmy looked at me again, and I felt as though I were peering at my own reflection. "Now I know in part; then I shall understand fully, even as I have been fully understood.'"

I thought how nice to be fully, and finally, understood.

He shut the Bible and put it on the night stand. "'So faith, hope, love abide, these three,'" he quoted, "'but the greatest of these is love.'"

Jimmy gazed into my eyes for a long time, and I felt a surge of longing for him. I felt my cheeks get hot, and looked away. But he took my hand and said, "Paul, let's pray together."

"Right now?" I said, a little surprised. "Here?"

"Yes." He pulled me off my bed and I got on my knees facing his bunk. He knelt beside me and clasped his hands in prayer, his shoulder lightly grazing mine.

"Dear God," he prayed, "help us abide in the love of Jesus, which surpasseth all understanding. Support us in developing a deeply spiritual friendship, so that our works, our faith, and our love will reflect all that is good and holy and true. In the name of Our Lord and Saviour, Jesus Christ, Amen."

I felt very moved by his prayer, and kept my eyes closed, feeling his warmth beside me. I didn't want this moment to end, but finally opened my eyes and looked shyly at him. He smiled and put his arm around my shoulder and gave it a squeeze. Just then, my penis rolled over. I clasped my hands as tight as I could to keep from getting aroused.

I condemned myself for turning even this innocent affirmation of our holy friendship into carnal desire. Luckily, he seemed not to notice my discomfort. He tousled my hair and said, "Good night, chum."

"Good night, Jimmy."

He blew out the lantern scooted under the covers. I got into my own bed and lay there for a long while, still in the darkness, listening to him breathe.

24: Reclaiming America

Early the next morning, the Rev bounced into the cabin and turned on the lights. "Let's get a move on!" he shouted, jovially. Jackson peered out from under his covers. It was still dark outside. He groaned, then let the blankets fall back over his face. Perry, who commonly slept flat on his back with his arms to his side all night long, raised his hands and stretched. Jimmy and I swung our legs onto the floor, facing each other. I grabbed my pants and placed them over my lap to hide my morning hard-on, which peeked through my shorts.

"No time for breakfast; we've got donuts and a thermos of hot chocolate for the trip. Just throw on your clothes, grab your suitcases, and let's get cracking!"

Jackson, still groggy and ill-tempered, stumbled into the bathroom. We quickly got dressed and loaded up the van. Ruth stood outside, fussing with Sheila's hair, until Sly lost his patience. "Suffering Jehosephat, will you just get in the van!" Ruth sat up front with Sly, and the rest of us piled into the two bench seats in back.

I asked Jimmy, "Who was Jehosaphat, anyway?"

"He was the King of Judah, who wiped out the last of the male cult prostitutes," Jimmy explained. "The story's in Kings."

I was sorry I asked. We ate our donuts and sipped hot chocolate on our way south over the Golden Gate Bridge.

*   *   *

Draped across the back of the stage at the Anaheim Convention Center was a huge American flag with a wooden Cross over the stripes. Above the flag hung a banner: "FAMILY RIGHTS FOREVER, GAY RIGHTS NEVER!"

At the opening convocation, the audience rose as one mass, and put their right hands over their hearts:

"I pledge allegiance to the Christian flag, and to the Saviour, for whose Kingdom it stands, one Saviour, crucified, risen, and coming again, with life and liberty for all who believe."

Jackson leaned over to whisper, "And everlasting hellfire for those who don't." He indicated with his thumb the crowd that pushed and shoved against the glass doors. A noisy demonstration of gay protesters jostled the police lines and waved signs like "Take a Homo to Lunch" and "Support the Separation of Church and State." They blew whistles and shouted "Self-Hating Fags!" Jimmy and I looked over our shoulders, but Sly told us to ignore them.

The title of the opening speech was "The New Civil War," by Jon Edwards, the head of RELEASE. A bald and portly man with glasses, he looked like anyone's grandfather. He wore a gray suit with a tie tack in the shape of a fish.

"This is a time of turmoil for God's Country," he began. "A time of troubles, in which all good Christians shall be sorely tested. God is using AIDS, floods, hurricanes, earthquakes, and firestorms to punish America for tolerating homosexuality." He paused for a moment to let this sink in, then continued.

"This judgment is not just my opinion; it's Biblical prophecy. Listen to Jude 7: 'Just as Sodom and Gomorrah indulged in unnatural lust, so are they set forth as an example, suffering the vengeance of eternal fire.'

"Remember: God gave us Ten Commandments, not ten suggestions." He glared at the assembly, the lights flashing on his spectacles. "Partial obedience is disobedience!

"America is at Ground Zero in the battle between God and Satan. You are footsoldiers in a Civil War of Spiritual Values versus the damnable darkness of Satanic intrigue, blasphemy, and homolust."

Here the Pastor gestured toward the crowd of queers clamoring at the doors: "See how these unrepentant homosexuals cavort about, singing and laughing, parading their licentiousness in front of innocent school children, spending their time on vanities, on pleasures, in contemptible debauchery."

From outside, we could hear the gays' chants and drums as they danced in circles and flaunted their half-naked bodies. Jackson craned his neck around to get a better look.

"Jude describes the deadly consequences of perversion: 'These are the blemishes on their love feasts, as they boldly carouse together: waterless clouds; fruitless trees in late autumn, twice dead, uprooted; wild waves of the sea, casting up the foam of their shame; wandering stars for whom the nether gloom of darkness has been reserved forever.'

"To the victors of this final combat go the spoils of our children!" he thundered. "Shall we allow America, in all her majesty and glory, to sink in complacency, to wallow in the filth and mire of moral degeneracy, and slide down that slick and slimy, slippery slope toward Sodom?"

The audience shouted with one voice, "NO!"

"Listen to Romans: 'Claiming to be wise, they became fools...They were filled with all manner of wickedness, evil, covetousness, malice. Full of envy, murder, strife, deceit, malignity, they are gossips, slanderers, haters of God, insolent, haughty, boastful, inventors of evil, foolish, heartless, and ruthless.'"

I felt light-headed just trying to keep up with the endless procession of these abhorrent vices. Then Jackson tugged at my sleeve. I looked outside and saw a circle of hunky guys lift a drag queen high in the air. She wore a glittering tiara and a dress of rainbow-colored sequins. As she rose on the shoulders of the bare-chested men, she blew kisses to the crowd, which hooted and hollered in approval.

But Pastor Edwards tried to reign in our drifting attention. "Deuteronomy warns us not to be fooled: 'Their vine is the vine of Sodom…their grapes are the grapes of gall, their clusters are bitter. Their wine is the poison of dragons, and the cruel venom of asps.'"

Jackson was still rubber-necking at the circus going on outside. Sly told him to turn around and pay attention. Jackson obeyed, but his eyes glazed over as the pastor continued his endless litany of sin and degradation.

"Let there be not the slightest doubt in your minds: the wrath of God burns against them—and against us, for tolerating their folly in our midst!"

Then Pastor Edwards pointed directly at me. "Do not think you are safe from God's fiery rage!" I flinched. Why me? "You are all citizens of that city which is so full of filthiness and abomination before God. You have committed those abominations, and have sorely provoked God. Though you may have reformed and now show a smooth face to the world, you are the impure inhabitants of Sodom!"

I looked at Jimmy, terrorized. Could God see into our hearts, and know that despite our repenting, we were still Sodomites? Jimmy reached over and squeezed my hand. I felt comforted at first, but then realized how holding hands might look to others, much less God. I felt a burning shame sear my face, and pulled my hand away.

"O sinner! Consider the danger you are in: God suspends you over the pit of hell, much as one dangles a spider, or some loathsome insect, over the flame. It is a wide and bottomless pit, a furnace full of the fire of wrath: you hang by a slender thread, with the flames of divine fury flashing about it, and ready every moment to singe it, and burn it asunder.

"God will be so far from pitying you when you cry out to Him, He will only laugh and mock. He will not only hate you, but He will hold you in the utmost contempt; no place shall be thought fit for you but under His feet: 'I will tread them in mine anger, and trample them in my fury!'" he shouted, and slammed his fist on the lectern.

Jackson woke with a start. "Whuzzup?" he asked.

"Fire will roast and blister you with a sizzling blaze surmounting the agony of all the other tortures put together," he continued, his face contorted and filled with blood. "This rampage of fire will cause you to feel the bite of asps, the teeth of lions, the bile of dragons, the hail of rocks, the terror of the rack, the dislocation of joints, the twisting of sinews, and the rending of nerves!"

He narrowed his eyes and wagged a finger of warning. "The wise and selective hellfire can detect the malice of each sin. It will inflict excruciating torment on the organ responsible! The fiery furnace of hell will distinguish a common killer from a patricide, your ordinary adulterer from incest, a fornicator from a sodomite!" I felt an electric jolt to my groin, and shifted uncomfortably in my seat.

Here a gleam came into his eye, as he relished the righteous rage of an incensed and irascible God: "'The teeth of wild beasts, scorpions, serpents, and the sword, punish the wicked to destruction,'" he declared. "Thick smoke, molten lead, boiling oil, burning cauldrons, lakes of fire—all of these await you in everlasting perdition! In the dark, caustic fumes of this eternal inferno, the wicked will weep and wail and gnash their teeth!"

Rocking back and forth, Pastor Edwards jabbed his finger at the audience and ended his sermon with a final admonition that scared the bejesus out of me: "Then you shall groan, then you shall weep, then you shall sigh, but it will be too late! Even your tears shall be tears of fire that will burn your eyes, scorch your cheeks, singe the very buttress of your soul, again and again and again, from here to eternity, for ever and ever, World without End, Amen."

25: Walk Like a Man

After the convocation, I was rattling in my boots. My palms were sweaty, and I felt feverish from all the pyrotechnical descriptions of blazing hellfire. Perry was still in his seat, crying, and Sly sat next to him, his arm around his shoulder, trying to comfort him. I glanced at the demonstrators waving their placards outside the glass doors, and imagined them being swallowed up in a cauldron of fire. Jimmy noticed me looking at them, and rubbed my back.

As much as I yearned for his touch, I shrugged him off and looked down at my program. Our testimonial with Sly wasn't until this afternoon, so we had some time to look around. The schedule announced various workshops throughout the day. Jackson and Sheila peered over our shoulders. "What's next?" Jackson said.

There were the usual scientific presentations about Reparative Therapy: "Overcoming Homosexuality," "Healing for the Homosexual," and "Homosexuality—Its Cause and Its Cure." Then we had a choice of "Crisis in Masculinity," 'Makeovers for Butches," and "How to Talk to a Former Homosexual."

"Let's go to this one," Jackson said. He pointed to "Walk Like a Man." "'How to sit, walk, and talk like a man,'" he read. "Doesn't that sound fun?"

"Better than Makeovers for Butches," Sheila said. All four of us decided to go. We left poor Perry with Ruth and Sly.

* * *

"Men mustn't cross legs knee over knee, it's too effeminate." This total queen named Bob wore sideburns with a thin moustache and demonstrated the pose at one end of the Starlight Room. He interlaced his fingers and sat with one knee over the other, then arched his eyebrows and pursed his lips. A titter went through the room, which was filled with young men like ourselves gawking over each other's shoulders.

"Occasionally it's okay to sit ankle over ankle." He stretched out his legs and put one foot over the other. "But a real man crosses ankle over knee." He grasped hold of one ankle and put it firmly on the other knee. "That's how men sit."

Then he asked for a volunteer. Jackson immediately raised his hand. "I'll do it!" He raced up to the front of the room.

Jimmy and I looked at each other. "This we gotta see," he said.

"What's your name?"

"Jackson."

"Hi, Jackson. Where are you from?"

"San Francisco."

A salacious "Ooh" went through the crowd.

"The Belly of the Beast, huh?"

"Mm hmm. I guess."

"Well, Jackson, I'm going to give you a little test."

"What happens if I fail? Do I get spanked?"

Everyone giggled.

Bob looked a little uncomfortable, but forged ahead. He handed Jackson three books: *Satan's Seven Schemes*, *Defeating Dark Angels*, and *The Spiritual Warrior's Prayer Guide*. "How should you carry these books?"

Jackson cradled them in the crook of his arm and clasped them to his chest. A snicker went through the crowd. Bob said, "Tsk, tsk," and took back the books. "Now, look at your fingernails."

Jackson held out his hand, palm facing away, fingers spread. Someone let out a yip.

"Please be quiet until Jackson has a chance to complete all the items," Bob said. "Now, check the sole of your shoe."

Jackson lifted his foot behind him and peered over his shoulder. The man next to me, who looked like a football player, let out a loud guffaw, then covered his mouth.

"Now, put your hand on your hip."

Jackson stood with the back of his wrist on his hip, and lifted his chin in a queeny pose. The whole crowd laughed.

"Can anyone point out what Jackson is doing wrong?"

This willowy boy raised his hand and stepped forward. He took the books from Bob and said, "First of all, men hold their books at their side, not their chest." He held the books at his thigh, then gave them back to Bob. "And they always look at their fingernails like this." He held his hand palm facing him and curled his fingers. "If you step on something obnoxious, you bend your knee in front of you, not behind you, to check your shoe." He lifted his left leg over his knee, and peered at the sole of his shoe.

"And a real man would never put the back of his wrist against his hip. You place both hands on your hips, palm-inward, fingers forward, thumbs back, like this. Or, you can tuck your thumbs inside the top of your pants, letting your fingers drape over your belt."

Bob said, "Thank you, Jeffrey. What Jeffrey just demonstrated is a very manly pose. From this pose, you can lift your chin and greet your friends. When you shake hands, give the other man a firm squeeze with a masculine handshake—not a limp fish! Try nodding at each other as you shake hands and say, 'Dude,' or 'Yo.'"

Bob asked us to break into pairs and practice posing with our partners. Jackson and the one other black guy in the room shook hands by grabbing each other's thumbs, sliding off the ends of their fingers, then they whirled around and slapped each other's palms.

Jimmy and I walked by each other, glancing at our nails by keeping our fingers curled. We stopped and checked the bottom of our shoes. Jimmy sat down and placed his ankle over his knee, then clasped his hands behind his head, like Sly. I looked over at him, my thumbs stuck in the top of my pants. "Yo," I said.

"Dude," Jimmy replied, lifting his chin. "How 'bout them Giants?"

He reached out to shake my hand, when Jackson let out a war whoop: "'Niners!" We looked at him, nearly doubled over, clenching his fist. "Forty-fuckin' 'Niners!"

Suddenly everyone was silent, staring at Jackson. Oops. Maybe that was a little too macho, even for this crowd. We quickly exited, then leaned against the wall in the hallway and busted out laughing.

"Dude!" Jimmy said.

"'Niners!" shouted Jackson.

"Yo!" I said, and we slapped each others' hands.

Sheila shook her head. "Must be a guy thing," she said.

* * *

Afterward, we went wandering around the conference. Jackson wanted to go to the souvenir store. They had all kinds of born-again paraphernalia: buttons, T-shirts, bumper-stickers, tapes, and books.

We found buttons sporting the following slogans:

"Don't Be the Boo-Boo Bird in God's Flock of Angels."
"Seven Days Without Prayer Makes One Weak."
"In Order to Get to Hell You Have to Step Over Jesus."
"Know fear—Fear of the Lord is the Beginning of Knowledge."

We also found a few bumper stickers:

"One on God's Side is a Majority."
"Let Jesus Fix Your Achy Breaky Heart."
"Sodom and Gomorrah had Gays in the Military."

"Turn or Burn, Fly or Fry, Live or Die."
"Make Straight the Way of the Lord—John 1:23."

Then we took turns holding up T-shirts for each other. One had "America, One Nation Under God" printed across the top, with a flag-draped bald eagle engulfed in flames. Below was a list of the moral challenges facing the U.S.: "Abortion, AIDS, special rights for homos, drug abuse, gangs, ban on prayer, sexual promiscuity, violent crime, gun control."

Sheila held up one that showed a devil with his pitch-fork leering out at the viewer: "You Can't Walk with God If You Run with the Devil."

Jackson said, "Yo!" and held up "Worship the Best or Die Like the Rest" in Harley Davidson script.

Jimmy showed us "The Lord's Gym," which showed Jesus doing push-ups with a cross on his back labeled "The Sins of the World." Underneath was the challenge, "Bench press this!"

I found a sweatshirt for a Varsity Wrestling Team, showing two wrestlers on the front, and on the back, a quote from Ephesians 6:12—"For our wrestling is not against flesh and blood opponents, but against the Principalities, against the Powers, the Worldly Rulers of this Present Darkness, the Spiritual Hosts of Wickedness in the Heavenly Spheres."

The book table held an assortment of titles with dire warnings of the coming Troubles. We glanced through *Dealing With the Devil*, *The Believer's Guide to Spiritual Warfare*, and *Are Homosexuals Security Risks?*

Jackson said it was time for us to meet up with Sly and Ruth for our testimonials. The Rev's workshop was called, "A Virtually Real Approach Healing from Sexual Brokenness." It was being held in the Celestial Auditorium.

Unaccustomed to speaking before large audiences, I felt nervous. We'd all worked on our speeches the previous week. I wrote down a few notes and figured that would help get me by, but I can't say I was looking forward to the ordeal. The Rev said it would be good for our souls to confess our salvation and progress towards sexual healing before such an important assembly.

We sat up on the dais with Ruth and Sly. Ruth began with a historical overview of previous approaches, most of which we had already tried: Orgasmic Reorientation, Covert Sensitization, and Aversive Therapy.

Then the Rev outlined his new treatment with slides from his laptop projected on the screen. He showed a diagram of the Virtual Reality machine and gave a technical description of the software he had developed to run his new program.

By this time, people were starting to nod off. It was even hard for me to keep up with his explanation, and I'd actually been through it.

Finally he said, "But of course, the proof's in the pudding. I have with me today some fine, upstanding ex-gays to testify on the efficacy of this new procedure, which will revolutionize the treatment of homosexuals."

He introduced us, and we took turns making brief statements at the podium. Perry went first, followed by Jackson and Sheila, giving testimonials very similar to our shares at HomoAnon. Jimmy, since he was new, decided to pass. Sly seemed flustered by this, since he had such grand notions for us as a team. But he let it drop, and turned to me.

To tell the truth, I didn't exactly feel ready, either, since I wasn't sure if I was really cured. But it seemed to mean so much to Sly that I didn't want to disappoint him.

I stepped up to the microphone and looked out over the audience, which was full of mostly middle-aged male treatment providers. "Hi. My name is Paul. I just wanted to say that after this treatment, any desire I previously had for the lifestyle has faded away from me. I feel released from sexual brokenness." A thunderous applause greeted my claim.

I blushed and said, "In all honesty, I can't say I'm ready to get married." Here the audience laughed good-naturedly, I suppose because I'd expressed a red-blooded reluctance to getting tied down. "But through the Grace of our Lord and Savior, I've been born again in the Spirit and the Life Everlasting, Amen."

"Amen!" echoed from the crowd, but this was the last friendly overture to greet us.

Sly opened up the meeting for questions. A stout man with white hair dressed in a blue leisure suit stood up. "Reverend Slocock, can you describe for us your rationale for using images of naked bodies in this procedure? It seems to me that your treatment borders dangerously close to purveying pornography."

Nods and murmurs rippled through the audience.

"I'm glad you asked that," Sly said. "There is an element of enticement, I agree, but it is in the service of re-orienting the subject's libidinal desires to the correct object. We have to recognize the power of animal instincts. We hope, of course, once the re-orientation is secure, to re-channel the libido to a more spiritual plane."

There was some grumbling through the crowd. It seemed that his presentation was not going as well as he had hoped. Members of the audience sat with their feet planted firmly on the floor, their arms crossed.

"Any other questions?" The room was silent.

"Well, you're welcome to come up afterwards and talk to me in person. I only regret we weren't able to bring the whole kit and kaboodle along with us; some of you could have tried it out and seen for yourselves."

People talked in pairs under their breath as they quickly filed out of the room. No one came up to us to ask any questions. So much for scads of new contracts for his Virtually Real Sexual Re-Orientation Machine.

Sly looked strangely defeated. I didn't know what to say. "I think it helped me," I said, trying to reassure him.

He touched my cheek with his hand. "You're a fine boy," he said. Then he packed up his laptop and left the auditorium.

26: David and Goliath

Sly said we'd take off early the next morning, and not stick around for the final plenary session. "The whole ex-gay movement has been taken over by Philistines," he claimed. "We don't have time for their machinations. We might as well go back to the ranch and carry on our noble labors."

Sly bunked with Perry and Jackson. Sheila stayed with Ruth, and I was assigned a room with Jimmy so I could look after him. "He's so new, I'd like you to keep an eye on him," Sly said. "There are so many ineptly treated homosexuals roaming the halls tonight, I'm afraid he might give way to temptation. We wouldn't want to chance a fall, would we?" I shook my head, and Sly patted my shoulder. "There's a good fellow."

Jimmy and I took our stuff into the room. My heart leapt to discover there was only one queen-size bed. I said, "There must be some mistake."

"What?" asked Jimmy.

"There's only one bed."

"I think I can handle it," Jimmy said, unpacking his knapsack.

"No, I better check." I went to the front desk, but all the rooms were booked. The clerk asked me if I wanted a rollaway. "Uh, sure. That would be fine."

"It's an extra thirty dollars."

"Oh. Okay." I pulled out my wallet, but I didn't have enough money. "Uh, never mind."

The guy smirked, like he knew what this convention was all about. Could he sense my own ambivalence? "Suit yourself," he said.

I thought of asking Sly, but I didn't want him to think I doubted my own ability to resist temptation. After all, I'd been through his treatment upteen times. Anyway, just because you sleep in the same bed doesn't mean anything has to happen.

I went back to the room. Jimmy looked up from unpacking. "Any luck?" I shook my head. "Well, if it's any reassurance, I wasn't planning to pounce on you."

"Oh, I wasn't worried about that," I lied. "I just roll over a lot. It's hard for me to get to sleep sometimes."

"Oh, don't worry about me. I sleep like a log."

It wasn't really him I was worried about.

I put on my pajamas in the bathroom. When I came out, Jimmy hopped into bed wearing only his shorts. I turned my eyes away from his chest, which reminded me of the image I'd made love to in Sly's Virtual Reality machine: well-developed muscles sliding under a satiny olive skin, a few dark hairs surrounding his nipples. Then I remembered the awful vision of Satanic tortures which followed, and steeled myself to resist temptation.

I pulled back the covers and sat down, facing away from him. I swung my feet onto the bed and leaned against the headboard, then gingerly pulled the covers up to my chest.

Jimmy reached over to his left and pulled a Gideon Bible out of the drawer. "Ever read the story about David and Goliath?" he asked.

I said I'd heard of it, of course, but I'd never read it.

"It's a cool story, actually. Goliath challenged Saul's army to pick one of their finest soldiers to fight him—whichever side lost would become servants to the other. But Goliath was a giant."

"How big was he?"

"Let's take a look." Jimmy opened the Bible to First Samuel 17 and scanned the lines. "Here he is: 'His height was six cubits and a span.'"

"What's a cubit?"

"A cubit's the length of a forearm—" he held his arm up next to my face, his biceps forming a bulge. I thought I was going to swoon. "About eighteen inches on a good-sized man. A span is the measure from the tip of your thumb to the end of your little finger—" he stretched out his hand, his little finger nearly touching my nose. "About nine inches."

I made some mental calculations. "So Goliath's around nine foot, nine? No wonder they called him a giant."

"Really. Listen to this description: 'He had a helmet of bronze on his head, and he was armed with a coat of mail, and the weight of the coat was five thousand shekels of bronze.'"

"How much is a shekel?"

"A shekel's about half an ounce. Let's see—" He got out a pencil and made some calculations on the hotel stationery. "His coat of mail was over a hundred and fifty pounds."

"Wow."

"Plus, 'he had greaves of bronze upon his legs'—that's armor for below the knee—'and a javelin of bronze slung between his shoulders. And the shaft of his spear was like a weaver's beam, and his spear's head weighed six hundred shekels of iron—' almost twenty pounds. Then Goliath said, 'Choose a man for yourselves, and let him come down to me. If he is able to fight with me and kill me, then we will be your servants; but if I prevail against him and kill him, then you shall be our servants and serve us.' Seems pretty reasonable, right? But the Israelites were quaking in their sandals."

"So how did they end up picking David?"

"David was a youth who acted as a go-between, bringing food to his brothers on the front lines. One day, Goliath appeared again and repeated his challenge. David said, 'Who is this uncircumcised Philistine, that he should defy the armies of the living God?' Then his brother scolded him for leaving his sheep unattended and coming down to watch the battle. But David told Saul that he'd fight Goliath: 'Let no man's heart fail because of him; your servant will go and fight this Philistine.'

"Of course, Saul dismissed him as a mere shepherd boy, whereas Goliath had been a soldier all his adult life. But David told him he had often rescued his lambs from predators: 'Your servant has killed both lions and bears; and this uncircumcised Philistine will be one of them.' Then Saul said to David, 'Go, and the Lord be with you!'

"'Saul clothed David with his armor; he put a helmet of bronze on his head, and clothed him with a coat of mail... Then David said to Saul, "I cannot go with these; for I am not used to them." And David put them off.'"

"He took off all his armor?"

"He was a shepherd, and the armor got in his way. 'Then he took his staff in his hand, and chose five smooth stones from the brook...His sling was in his hand, and he drew near to the Philistine.'

"Of course, Goliath just laughed at him, 'for he was but a youth, ruddy and comely in appearance. And the Philistine said to David, "Am I a dog, that you come to me with sticks?"' He cursed him and said, 'Come to me, and I will give your flesh to the birds of the air and to the beasts of the field.'

"Then David said, 'You come to me with a sword and a spear and a javelin; but I come to you in the name of the Lord of hosts, the God of the armies of Israel, whom you have defied.'

"So they went at each other: 'And David put his hand in his bag and took out a stone, and slung it, and struck the Philistine on his forehead; the stone sank into his forehead, and he fell on his face to the ground...Then David ran and stood over the Philistine, and took his sword and drew it out of its sheath, and killed him, and cut off his head with it. When the Philistines saw that their champion was dead, they fled.'"

"Wow," I said. "But weren't the Philistines supposed to become their servants?"

"That was the idea, but they took off. Saul was so impressed with David, that he brought him back to his own home. Jonathan, Saul's son, was very much taken with him: 'The soul of Jonathan was knit to the soul of David…Then Jonathan made a covenant with David, because he loved him as his own soul. And Jonathan stripped himself of his robe and gave it to David, and his armor, and even his sword and his bow and his girdle. And David went out and was successful wherever Saul sent him.'"

27: Jonathan and David

Jimmy continued with the story. "The only trouble was, David was getting too popular. 'The women came out of all the cities of Israel, singing and dancing, to meet King Saul, with timbrels, with songs of joy, and with three-stringed instruments. And the women sang to one another as they made merry, "Saul has slain his thousands, And David his ten thousands." And Saul was very angry, and this saying displeased him; he said, "They have ascribed to David ten thousands, and to me they have ascribed thousands; and what more can he have but the Kingdom?" And Saul eyed David from that day on.'"

"Why was he so jealous?" I asked.

"He figured David was after his throne. 'And on the morrow an evil spirit from God rushed upon Saul, and he raved within his house, while David was playing his lyre, as he did day by day. Saul had his spear in his hand; and Saul cast the spear, for he thought, "I will pin David to the wall." But David evaded him twice.'"

I said, "Why didn't David realize what was happening?"

"To allay his suspicions, Saul cooked up this scheme to marry him off to one of his daughters. 'Saul thought, "Let me give her to him, that she may be a snare for him, and that the hand of the Philistines may be against him."'"

"Since David was just a poor man, he was impressed that Saul would choose him to be his son-in-law, but he had no wedding gift. Saul's servants reassured him, saying, 'The King desires no marriage present except a hundred foreskins of the Philistines, that he may be avenged of the King's enemies.'"

"Oh I get it," I said. "He was setting him up."

"That's right. But little did Saul realize that David could pull it off. 'David arose and went, along with his men, and killed two hundred of the Philistines; and David brought their foreskins.'"

I winced. "That is so gross."

"Well, it was a lot easier proof to bring home than two hundred heads."

"But wait a minute," I said. "Michelangelo's David is uncircumcised."

"That's 'cause in Europe, only Jews were circumcised."

"But wasn't David a Jew?"

"Yeah, that's true. Maybe Michelangelo just liked uncut guys." Jimmy nudged my arm with his elbow.

I felt a surge in my own uncut member, and blushed.

"So anyway, whenever David went out into battle, he had one success after another, till Saul felt very threatened by him and wanted to kill him. 'But Jonathan, Saul's son, delighted much in David.' So Jonathan warned David, 'Saul my father seeks to kill you,' and he told him to hide.

"'And Jonathan spoke well of David to Saul his father, and said to him, "Let not the King sin against his servant David…because his deeds have been of good service to you…You saw it, and rejoiced; why then will you sin against innocent blood by killing David without cause?"

"'And Saul hearkened to the voice of Jonathan; Saul swore, "As the Lord lives, he shall not be put to death."' So Jonathan reassured David, and everything was back to normal. 'And there was war again; and David went out and fought with the Philistines, and made a great slaughter among them, so that they fled before him.' Saul was still jealous of David's success. He tried to pin him again with his spear while he played the lyre. That night, David's wife told him he must flee, or Saul would kill him. She made up his bed with a pillow of goats' hair so he could get away.

"Then David told Jonathan that Saul was still trying to kill him, but Jonathan said he didn't think so, because Saul hadn't said anything about it to him. 'But David replied, "Your father knows well that I have found favor in your eyes; and he thinks, Let not Jonathan know this, lest he be grieved."' Then Jonathan was convinced that David was in danger. He said, 'Whatever you say, I will do for you...And Jonathan made David swear again by his love for him; for he loved him as he loved his own soul.'"

"How about that," I said. "For the love of David, Jonathan was willing to betray his own father."

Jimmy smiled. "That's right. So that night, Jonathan told Saul that David had gone to Bethlehem to celebrate the holidays with his relatives. Saul was angry with Jonathan for letting David escape. 'You son of a perverse, rebellious woman, do I not know that you have chosen David to your own shame?...For as long as David lives upon the earth, neither you nor your kingdom shall be established. Therefore send and fetch him to me, for he shall surely die.' Saul was afraid that David would usurp the throne and keep Jonathan from becoming King.

"'Then Jonathan answered Saul his father, "Why should he be put to death? What has he done?" But Saul cast his spear at him to smite him; so Jonathan knew that his father was determined to put David to death.

"'In the morning Jonathan went out into the field to his appointment with David, and with him a little lad. And he said to his lad, "Run and find the arrows which I shoot." As the lad ran, he shot an arrow beyond him...Jonathan called after the lad and said, "Is not the arrow beyond you?" And Jonathan called after the lad, "Hurry, make haste, stay not."'

"Because they had prearranged this signal, David knew that he must flee for his life. 'And as soon as the lad had gone, David rose from beside the stone heap and fell on his face to the ground...and they kissed one another, and wept with one another.' Then Jonathan said to David, 'Go in peace, forasmuch as we have sworn both of us in the name of the Lord, saying, The Lord shall be between me and you, and between my descendants and your descendants, forever.'"

"So David escaped?" I asked. Jimmy nodded. "Was that the last time they ever saw each other?"

"No. A bit later, Saul ambushed the priests who were hiding David. Jonathan found David in the wilderness, and told him that he would be King over Israel.

"Then Saul came into the mountains looking for David, and went inside a cave to relieve himself, the same cave where David was hiding. And David thought he might kill him, but instead, he spared him and swore his allegiance to him. Saul had a change of heart, so long as David would not keep Saul's sons from inheriting his Kingdom.

"But then Saul went after him again, and David spared him one more time; but he no longer trusted him, and fled to the land of the Philistines, where Saul 'sought for him no more.'"

"God, it's about time," I said.

"Then later, the Philistines made a raid on Israel, but they would not let David join them, afraid he might switch sides and fight for King Saul. During the ensuing battle, the Philistines killed Saul and his sons, including Jonathan."

"They killed Jonathan?"

"Yes. And when David learned of it, he 'took hold of his clothes, and rent them...and they mourned and wept and fasted.' Listen to David's lament over his beloved friend:

> "'Thy glory, O Israel, is slain upon thy high places!
> How the mighty have fallen!
> Saul and Jonathan, beloved and lovely!
> In life and in death they were not divided;
> they were swifter than eagles,
> they were stronger than lions.
> How the mighty have fallen
> in the midst of the battle!
> Jonathan lies slain upon thy high places.
> I am distressed for you, my brother Jonathan;
> very pleasant have you been to me;

your love to me was wonderful,
passing the love of women.
How the mighty have fallen,
and the weapons of war perished!'"

"How sweet they were to each other," I said, tears in my eyes. I leaned against Jimmy's shoulder, and he put his arm around me.

28: Passing the Love of Women

We sat for a few moments, my head on his shoulder, his arm across my back. He ran his fingers through my hair and softly hummed. I felt relaxed and comforted, but this did not last long. Very soon I was aware of his chin resting on my head, my cheek next to his bare chest, and I started to get aroused.

I scooted up in bed and clasped my knees to my chest.

"Are you all right?"

I nodded. "I'm fine. That was such a sad story." I rested my cheek on my knee.

He stroked my back. "They really did care for each other."

I sighed. I was so confused. I knew what was happening; or thought I did. I remembered Madame Blavatsky's prophecy—that I would be tempted against my better judgment; that I must trust my instincts, lest I be led astray. And yet I felt my heart brim full of yearning; not only with carnal desire (though I won't deny that), but also with what I thought was love. I'd had crushes of course on other boys, like Matt; and I'd had fun at the clubs giving guys a wank; but I'd never really ever been in love.

Did that make everything somehow different? Surely Jonathan and David were in love—Jonathan to the point where he was willing to defy his own father, the King! And although David got married, he declared his love for Jonathan had surpassed even the love of women.

I had to be honest with myself. I had yearned for this moment from the first second I laid eyes on Jimmy at the parade, his dark features so full of passion and fury. My outreach to the jail was little more than a sham. It's as though I had planned this seduction all along! Maybe that's not altogether true; all I knew in the beginning was that I wanted to be near him.

And here I made this big show about getting another bed. Otherwise this time I knew I wouldn't be strong enough to resist him. Yet I thrilled to the possibility that I would be overwhelmed—the flesh is so strong, my will so weak—confused and torn, vulnerable to his obvious lies that he cared for me. It was all a ploy, set in motion by Satan himself to tempt me. He knew my vulnerability; he could see it in my eyes, feel it beneath his fingertips when my skin responded to his touch. I should be angry with him, setting me up this way—or at myself, for allowing it.

My heart was thumping, afraid of what I was about to do, to allow to happen, not knowing what to say, when Jimmy spoke.

"Undermining your faith is the last thing I would desire," he said, as if reading my mind.

"What?"

"You don't have to speak, just look at me."

I glanced at him over my shoulder for a second, but I could not maintain eye contact. Then he took my face in his hands. I fell back against the pillows, and finally gazed into his eyes. He leaned on one elbow and rested his forearm across my chest. He smiled so sweetly and I felt such longing, I thought my heart would burst. A verse from the Song of Songs echoed through my mind: "O that he would kiss me, with the kisses of his lips!"

"You're a terrific guy," he said, tracing my lips with his finger. "And there is nothing I would like more than to kiss you, and hold you, and make love to you."

My penis leapt out of its foreskin. I thought, this is it. I closed my eyes, and saw flames flicker along the walls of the cave, yet I knew I could not resist a moment longer.

But then he pulled his hand away and said, "I have a confession to make." I could still feel him touching my lips, like phantom fingerprints. "I'm afraid I've entered your life under false pretenses."

"What? What do you mean?"

He sat up. "When you came to visit me in the jail, the idea entered my head that I would purposely try to seduce you."

"What?"

"All this ex-gay stuff is bullshit," he said. "I hate the hypocrisy and the lies, the self-deceit. I would prove to you that you were no more an ex-gay than I was. I wanted to have sex with you, but not because I cared for you. Because I wanted to humiliate you."

A part of me could not believe him—I knew he cared for me! Another part was relieved. Oh thank God, I'm saved! And yet I was strangely outraged. How dare he use me in so cynical a fashion! And still another thought: so?

I couldn't say any of these reactions, but only looked at him with a mixture of shock, dismay, and longing.

"It was all a scam! And when my first attempt didn't work, I pretended to go along by apologizing to Sly and joining Escape. Although I detested every minute of it: Ruth's idiotic bombast, Sly's hypocritical leers, it wasn't so hard for me to follow the program. That's how I was brought up. But I was willing to do it, merely to entice you, corrupt, debauch, and expose you in this ridiculous lie."

I turned away from him, a terrible lump in my throat. So that's all it was: all these confessions of love and deep gazes into my eyes were nothing but lies.

"Before I got to know you, I could easily have had you and dropped you in a minute, gloating at my conquest."

What a cur. "How could you?" I said. He took my hand, but I yanked it away, trembling.

"I think I might have succeeded, even now." He touched my shoulder, and I cringed. He's awfully sure of himself—but he was right. He could have seduced me in a minute.

"But then, hearing your naive questions in Bible study, going for walks with you through the meadows, laughing with you while putting lunch together or playing football with the guys, then shyly showering together afterward; and most of all, lying in the next bunk, night after night, watching you in the moonlight, listening to you breathe, seeing a lock of your brown hair fall across your eyes in innocent slumber, I began to care for you."

"Yeah, I'm sure," I said.

He struck the bed with his fist. "Damn! I should never have come on to you when I first came to Escape. Now you'll never believe me, no matter what I say!" He turned away and stifled a sob.

Seeing how overcome he was, I wanted to take him in my arms and reassure him. I reached out and touched his back.

"Don't touch me!" he said.

My hand flew back as though I'd been scorched.

"Don't you realize how you're torturing me?"

I'm torturing him?

He turned toward me with tears in his eyes. "Can't you see how much I want you, how much I've longed for you?"

I was stunned to hear him confess the same feelings that I felt for him.

"But I can't let myself be conquered by you under these ridiculous circumstances," he said.

"Why not?" I asked, shocked by my own boldness.

"We're at an ex-gay conference, for God's sake! This isn't how I want it to happen. I can't bear to have you think of me tempting you like the devil. I don't want to seduce you, then have you suffer a 'fall' and be so full of guilt and remorse that you reject me. I want you to want me, love me and cherish me, not to fear me."

My head was spinning. I felt so full of desire and pain; both deeply honored, yet horribly rejected. And yet suddenly released, too, from a terrible temptation—but I was no longer certain I wanted to be.

"Believe me," he said, "it's better this way." He got out of bed and hastily pulled on his pants.

"What are you doing?" I said.

"I've got to go."

"But why? It's all right. We don't have to do anything. I—I'll sleep on the floor."

"I can't stay here. It's agony for me, can't you see that?"

"But, what will I tell the others?"

"Tell them, tell them my mother is sick. Tell them I had to go back to work. Hell, I don't care. Tell them the truth!"

The truth? I thought, what truth? Which truth? I was so confused and afraid to let my love escape me, I could not even think. "When will I see you again?"

"I don't know. Maybe you won't. Maybe you should marry Ruth and live happily ever after."

"Marry Ruth!"

"Sure, Sly's got it all arranged." He looked at me as he threw on his shirt. "You didn't know?"

"No!" I said. "Why would I marry Ruth?"

"You haven't seen how she looks at you, caters to you, fawns over you?"

I shook my head, bewildered.

"Well whatever. Anyway, I'm out of here." He stuffed his remaining clothes in his knapsack and slung it over his shoulder. Then he bent over the bed and gave me a peck. "'Parting is such sweet sorrow,'" he said, caressing my cheek.

I wanted to bring him close, clasp him in my arms, engulf him forever, let the Devil do what he will. I tried to grasp his hand, but Jimmy sprang away from me and was out the door before I could say another word.

29: Homo Erectus

The next morning, Sly got us up early to check out and pack our stuff into the van. Of course everyone wondered what happened to Jimmy. I said he had family living in southern California and had gotten word that his mother was sick, so he went to visit her.

"He'll be back, won't he?" asked Perry, who had also grown fond of him.

"I guess so," I said. "I mean, sure he will." The Rev looked over his shoulder at me, no doubt suspecting something unseemly had happened, but I just leaned my chin on my palm and stared out the window as we pulled onto the highway.

I'd never felt so forlorn, bereft of joy, and hopeless about my quest for healing. I should have been glad that Jimmy was honest enough to admit his unscrupulous mission before something dreadful happened. I could have been seduced and abandoned, suffering a fall I might never have recovered from.

So why was I so miserable? The truth was, his confession put me in touch with my own true feelings for him—if anything, I loved him all the more. Yet it was impossible—we were both young men! It was against God's plan, it was obviously not meant to be. Here, in the midst of my fellow ex-gays was where I belonged, not in some sordid bar south of Market Street in San Francisco.

Then why wasn't I rejoicing at my narrow escape? It must be the Devil digging in his heels, turning everything good into sorrow, everything bad into some luminous temptation, luring me to my downfall. I thanked my lucky stars and my new-found faith that I had withstood this terrible test. But I felt a wrenching in my heart that I thought would rend my soul with longing.

We got on I-5 and headed north, passing the Matterhorn, whose peak could just be seen from the freeway. "Hey!" Jackson protested. "I thought we were going to Disneyland!"

"We don't have time for that," Sly snapped, and that was the end of it. Jackson slumped against the seat and sulked, grumbling to himself. Sly's promise of Disneyland, no doubt, was based on the assumption he'd have a slew of new contracts for his Virtual Reality treatment. He was probably ashamed to admit he didn't have enough money to take us.

We wound through the Grapevine, then plunged into the fog smothering the central valley like a blanket. Sly gripped the steering wheel, white-knuckled, fixated on the short stretch of visible highway, which unrolled like an endless gray ribbon in the thick tule fog. In contrast to the ride down, which was full of fun songs and word games, our trip home was tense, almost solemn.

At one point, trying to fathom the motives of the forces arrayed against him at the conference, we overheard Sly mutter to Ruth, "Who knows what evil lurks in the hearts of men?"

She just shook her head, when a small voice from the back of the van said quietly, "The shadow knows." The rest of us jerked around to discover Perry huddled in the back seat, gazing at the ceiling.

* * *

Back at the ranch, the Rev met with each of us to decompress from the conference. I was too ashamed to admit how close I had come to falling, although he might very well have been sympathetic, and even congratulated me on seeing through Jimmy's evil plan. But I decided not to tell, in hopes that Jimmy would have a change of heart and return to the fold. If

I admitted my own narrow escape, or told Sly about Jimmy's true feelings, I knew he would never allow him back into the program.

Luckily, Sly was so preoccupied with justifying his approach in the face of our recent debacle, that at first he didn't probe too much about what happened between me and Jimmy. And I was so saddened by Jimmy's leaving that I went along when Sly said I needed a deep tissue massage.

"I sense a sorrow in you," he said, which was hard for me to deny. "What you experience as deprivation is really the creaking adjustment of masculine realignment. Your multi-modal, Virtually Real experience helped exorcise the demons. Now it's time to go deeper into the core to make the vessel more receptive to its true spiritual nature."

Sly stood behind me and started massaging my neck and shoulders, which actually felt rather comforting, though I admit I fantasized about Jimmy's own sweet touch after he read me the story of Jonathan and David.

Then he had me lie down on my stomach, right on the floor in his office. He massaged my back, stroked my butt, and caressed the back of my legs, then turned me over. He lifted my knees and rolled each thigh between his palms, all the way down to my groin. This seemed a little odd, but I tried to relax and allow him to realign my deep tissues.

Then he took my arm in his lap. "You have nice biceps and triceps," he said, squeezing my muscles through the sleeve.

"Oh, my arms are so skinny," I said. "And my chest isn't very manly."

"Nonsense," he said. "Take off your shirt." I sat up and shyly unbuttoned my shirt. He helped me slip it off, and I lay down on my back. "You have a handsome chest," he said, running his hand over my nipples. "It's fine and strong—a little underdeveloped, perhaps, but we'll take care of that in no time. Remind me during P.E. to show you some exercises for your pecs. We'll have you do some Marine Corps push-ups."

He put his hand over my heart, then put my left hand over his own heart. Then he started to massage my chest. This was important, he said, to ease the heart pain. He opened his shirt and put my hand on his hairy breast. "This is the way to connect the masculine energies," he said. I felt a little squeamish, and drew my hand away. I sat up and rested my forearms on my knees.

Sly took his shirt off. "It's okay for men to touch. There's a natural skin-hunger in same-sex friendships."

I have to admit, I didn't mind the shoulder massage, but then he started asking me details about my sexual fantasies and previous experiences—stuff like, "What turns you on? What do you think of Jimmy? Did you see Jimmy naked at the conference?"

I wasn't sure how to answer these questions. I figured he was suspicious about what happened between us—and wondered what made Jimmy take off. So I was sort of vague in answering him, which of course he noticed right away.

He said, "Confessing will help you get over your unnatural tendencies."

"There really isn't anything to confess!" I blurted out, rather defensively. It was more or less the truth, but I felt guilty, even though nothing had happened. I guess I was still protecting Jimmy.

Then he stood up and took off his pants! This rather surprised me. He was naked except for his jockey shorts. "What—"

He dismissed my modesty and said, "Being naked is a way to desensitize the charge of being around another male body, so we can become just like brothers. Let's hug," he suggested. He pulled me off the floor, and gave me a full-body embrace, grinding his hips into mine. I couldn't help but notice he was getting an enormous erection. I've never been a size queen, but I must admit it attracted my attention, even though I also felt a little uneasy.

I tried to push away, but he held me tight. "Don't pay any attention if you notice me getting an erection," he said. "It's all right for heterosexual men to hug and have erections. It doesn't mean anything—it's just nature—as long as you don't act on it."

I wondered whether this was really supposed to be part of my treatment program. But I figured even if it was a little unorthodox, it wasn't going to kill me.

He finally let me go. "When you're regularly exposed to the male body, you'll come to think it's normal and not be turned on by it," he assured me. "It's called Systematic Desensitization." I guess in a way he was right, because I certainly wasn't turned on by him.

Then he suggested I take off my pants, "to free the circulation." He noticed my hesitation. "Are you doubting me?"

"Well, not exactly. I just don't understand why that should be necessary."

"Faith precludes doubt," he said. "Doubt is from the Devil. Put your trust in Jesus," he assured me.

This seemed pretty intimate to me, but I tried to be open-minded. After all, he's a counselor! He must know what he's doing. So I took off my pants, and then he offered me a full-body, nude massage. "Nude massage will help you get used to being naked with other men without it leading to sex."

"I think I'd just as soon keep my shorts on," I said.

"You're obviously suffering from a severe case of misapodysis—an extreme dislike of undressing in front of others. But suit yourself."

I lay down again, and he massaged my chest. Then, while passing his hands over my stomach and thighs, he grazed the outline of my penis through my shorts. "Genesis 17:9 says, 'Every male among you shall be circumcised.'"

I blushed. "I know, it's strange, but my parents were hippies and they didn't believe in doing anything unnatural."

"Let me have a look at it."

I sat up and backed away. "Uh, why? You've seen me in the shower."

"An unclean foreskin can lead to all kinds of complications," Sly said.

"Like what? I never had any problems."

"I don't mean to alarm you," he said, "but smegma is known to cause cancer of the cock."

He reached through the fly of my boxer shorts and took out my penis. "Let's take a look here." When he slid back my foreskin, I started to get an erection. I pulled away and turned over on my stomach, deeply embarrassed.

He waited for a moment, not saying anything. Then he leaned over me and pressed his hands along the length of my back. He gradually slipped his fingers under the band of my underwear and kneaded my buttocks. When he started to pull off my shorts, I turned over and sat up again. "What are you doing, Sly?"

"Listen to First Corinthians," Sly said. "Chapter 12, verse 24-25: 'But God has so adjusted the body, giving the greater honor to the inferior part, that there be no discord in the body, but that the members shall have the same care for one another." Sly reached over and touched my own member again through my shorts. "What would you like me to do?" he asked.

"Nothing," I said, and threw his hand off me.

"But look at you! You know you want some release."

It's true, I still had a partial erection. But I shook my head and kept my shorts on.

Again he quoted: "I Corinthians 12:26 tells us, 'If one member suffers, all suffer together; if one member is honored, all rejoice together.'"

I raised my knee self-protectively. Sly sat back on his haunches, and I could see the outline of his hard-on bulging against his briefs. He said, "First John 4 tells us, 'God is love, and he who abides in love abides in God, and God abides in him.'"

I couldn't really argue with that, but I wasn't sure what the point was.

He touched my foot and looked at me earnestly. "'Beloved, if God so loved us, we also ought to love one another.'"

I pulled my foot away and wrapped my arms around my knees.

"'There is no fear in love, but perfect love casts out fear,'" he continued. "'He who does not love, does not love God, for God is love.'"

He put his hand on my shoulder, but I shrugged him off. "You know," he said, obviously irritated, "you've got a real problem if you don't allow men to touch you—it shows that you're still caught by your desire, still fending it off."

I finally stood up and grabbed my pants. "There's nothing wrong with me!" I said, louder than I expected. I thrust my legs into my jeans and buttoned my fly. If anything, I thought, there was something wrong with him, but I held my tongue. Why did he keep pressing me for this kind of contact? This was getting just a little too weird.

"Please lower your voice," he said. "A simple release of built-up tension is not really queer. However, I'd prefer that you not tell the others because it could so easily be misinterpreted."

I shook my head. At that point I'd have agreed to anything just to get out of there.

"If you don't discharge the vital bodily fluids, they can back up and begin to stagnate. But it's up to you—"

"Well, no thanks," I said, and put on my shirt.

Sly looked very disappointed. "First John also tells us, 'If anyone says, "I love God," and hates his brother, he is a liar; for he who does not love his brother whom he has seen, how can he love God whom he has not seen? And this commandment we have from him, that he who loves God, should love his brother also.'"

"I don't hate you," I said. "I just don't feel comfortable with this." Looking back, I'm amazed that I needed to explain myself.

"You can't fool me," Sly said. He stood up and his tone suddenly turned ominous. "You're not as innocent as you pretend. Don't think I don't know what happened between you and Jimmy at the conference!"

"Nothing happened!" I shouted.

"Why did he leave, then?"

I couldn't answer him.

Sly hovered over me, menacingly. "I think it's about time you made a confession."

"We never had sex, all right?"

"You lusted after him in your heart, admit it!"

I was silent. He was right. But what did that have to do with any of this?

"After he spat in my face, I turned the other cheek by dropping the charges against him; I took him into my home, fed him, gave him the shirt off my back—all for you, since you had taken such a special interest in this renegade apostate. And this is the thanks I get?"

"We didn't do anything!"

"And you! You ingrate. You catamite. You gazooney, sodomite, man-lover!" Sly swung his shirt around in an arc, and shot his fists through his sleeves. His anger scared me. "If you want to continue with this program, you are grounded to these premises. You will not be allowed to work the street fairs or witness in San Francisco. If Jimmy comes back, there will be absolutely no communication between you. I will sleep in the bunkhouse myself to make sure there's no fooling around. Is that understood?"

I nodded, bewildered.

"Good!" he said. Then he turned and stormed out of his office, slamming the door behind him. It wasn't until a moment later I realized he had left without his pants.

30: Hunky Punky

I began to suspect there was something not quite right about Sly and Escape. So why didn't I just leave? That's a good question. I suppose because I felt responsible for the Rev's disappointment in me. Here he had rescued me off the street and offered me a place to stay, free of charge—all I had to do was give up my willful and stubborn attachment to same-sex attractions.

Maybe there was something I didn't fully understand about his methods—as queer and oddly self-serving as they sometimes appeared. After all, he was supposed to be an ordained minister, trained in pastoral counseling and reparative therapy for homosexuals. He must have been trying to show me that despite my protests to the contrary, I'm still trapped by my desires. Even though he was wrong about some of the particulars, he was right that I was in love with Jimmy, and I felt ashamed.

* * *

That afternoon, just before Bible study, our little group had gathered in the Fireside Room, and Jackson regaled us with this passage he found in Titus 1:12: "'One of themselves, a prophet of their own, said, "Cretans are always liars."' Think about it: if I'm a Cretan then I'm not telling the truth, which means I'm lying, so I am telling the truth about being a liar, which suggests I'm really not lying—"

By this time, we were all laughing, but he wouldn't let up: "Which means I was lying when I said I'm a liar, so I am a liar, only if I was lying about being a liar I must not really be lying—"

"Stop it!" Sheila squealed, holding her stomach.

"Because all Cretans are liars. So I was telling the truth. Which means I must be lying. So I was telling the truth. So I'm a liar—"

Just then Ruth walked in and we all tried to stifle it, which of course only made it worse. In response to our giggles, Ruth said, "I don't see any reason for this unnecessary mirth." Unable to contain ourselves any longer, we all burst out in loud guffaws.

Ruth looked miffed, as though we'd been laughing about her. "Ephesians 5:4 tells us, 'Let there be no filthiness, nor silly talk, nor levity, which are not fitting.'"

"It was in the Bible," Perry chortled, tears running down his cheeks. It was rare to see him so full of mirth.

"What was?" Ruth demanded.

"All Cretans are liars!" Sheila shrieked, and we totally lost it. Ruth just stared at us as if we'd all gone bonkers.

When she finally got us settled down, she brought up her lesson for the day, which had to do with proper sex roles. "If we followed the directives of the Bible, there would be none of the confusion we see today in sexual brokenness, promiscuity, and broken homes. First Peter 3:1 tells us very clearly how to get along with one another: 'You wives, be submissive to your husbands.'"

Jackson wagged his finger at Sheila, who stuck her tongue out at him.

Ruth, oblivious, continued. "Ephesians 4:23-24 informs us, 'For the husband is the head of the wife as Christ is the head of the church…As the church is subject to Christ, so let wives also be subject in everything to their husbands.'"

Sheila could contain herself no longer. "But what if he's an idiot? Or a drunk?"

"Like Noah," Perry said, quietly.

"Or a wife-beater?" I asked.

"Well," said Ruth, "I Peter 3:7 says, 'Likewise you husbands, live considerately with your wives, bestowing honor on the woman as the weaker sex.'"

"Well hey, that oughtta take care of it," Jackson said.

Sheila pinched her nose and pursed her lips, raising her eyebrows in a dainty, lady-like pose. Perry laughed. Ruth gave him a sharp look, and he stopped abruptly. Then Perry leaned over toward Jackson and pointed out another verse.

Jackson laughed and said, "Dude! That's the best verse you found yet!"

"What are you looking at? What is this needless merriment?" She yanked the Bible away from Jackson and peered at the pages.

"What was it?" I whispered. Jackson flipped through my Bible, then pointed to Timothy 2:12: "I permit no woman to teach or have authority over men; she is to keep silent."

When Ruth found the verse, her face turned pale with anger. She narrowed her eyes at Perry and Jackson, who covered their silly grins with their hands like schoolboys.

Just then, Sly burst into the room carrying a stack of magazines, looking rather wild-eyed. "Purveyors of perversity!" he shouted. "There's been some hunky punky going on around here!"

We all looked at each other, rather bewildered. Jackson raised his eyebrows at me and mouthed "Hunky punky?"

Ruth said, "Reverend, we are in the middle of our Bible Study."

Sly flung the magazines onto the coffee table. "I am shocked, shocked! to find the boys looking at porno!"

Copies of Honcho, Playguy, Mandate, and Freshmen slid across the slick surface and onto the floor. A Raunch magazine landed at Perry's feet. He stared at it fearfully and drew his legs up to his chair.

"I found this filth hidden under a mattress in the bunkhouse." He turned toward the guys and said, "I don't think you boys realize what you are playing with here. Homosexuality is in direct opposition to God.

Indulging in carnal homo-lust, even in fantasy, will put your entire spiritual life in jeopardy!"

He picked up the copy of Raunch and folded it in disgust. "In some respects," he continued, "it would almost be better if you were dead—yes, dead! than to continue with this despicable homosexual lifestyle!"

Ruth said, "Reverend! You can't mean that!"

"I have never been more serious in all my life," Sly insisted. "James 1:15—'When lust hath conceived it bringeth forth sin: and sin, when it is finished, bringeth forth death.' At least in physical death you can still have a spiritual resurrection, whereas indulging in homosexuality you are yielding yourselves to a spiritual death from which there is absolutely no recovery."

He waved the magazine in the air. "I demand to know who is responsible for trafficking and smuggling in this despicable, disgusting muck, this slime, this sludge, this vile obscenity!"

I looked down at the floor. Jackson, whose magazines they were, looked out the window. Although I doubt Perry even knew about them, he looked stricken.

"You refuse to confess?" he asked. "Even at the risk of eternal damnation?"

We were silent.

"Perry?"

Perry shuddered, and hugged his knees. He couldn't say a word.

"Paul?"

I shook my head.

"Jackson?"

Still looking out the window, Jackson said, "Ain't nobody don't know about no porno."

"Oh, is that so?" Sly said. "So where did this trash come from? Out of thin air?"

Jackson, indignant, turned and glared at Sly. "I ain't gonna sit here in no chair and let no half-ass preacher man tell me no lies about no hunky punky porno mags that no ex-faggots never seen or hid or knowed about no-how."

"Well fine," Sly said, and slapped his hand with the folded magazine. He turned to Ruth. "I've decided to take the boys to Nevada."

"No!" Ruth shouted. "Not Nevada!"

"Yes," the Rev nodded gravely. "Nevada."

I looked at Jackson. What in the world was this about?

Ruth stood up and spread her arms, as if to protect us. "Anything but Nevada!"

Jackson, always considering the financial angle, said, "Hey! We could go to Reno!"

Realizing something serious was up, I shook my head at him. He folded his arms and kept quiet.

Sly said, "I admit it's unorthodox, it's extreme, but it's an example of antistasis—preventing something far worse which would no doubt occur if we did not institute drastic measures immediately."

Ruth gasped. "You can't mean—Stallion Ranch?"

"Exactly," Sly said.

"No, no, no, no!" Ruth went down on her knees. "A thousand times, no!"

Jackson mouthed to me, "What's Stallion Ranch?"

I lifted my eyebrows and shrugged. Sheila looked wide-eyed, no doubt astounded at Ruth taking such a strong stand with her brother. Perry cowered in the corner.

"It's perverse!" Ruth continued. "It's depraved! It's lecherous, lascivious, and lewd!"

"Sometimes a man's gotta do what a man's gotta do. Just remember," Sly said, "I'm doing it for you."

"Not Paul!" Ruth pleaded. "Paul's doing fine!"

Jackson looked at me in surprise. I remembered Jimmy's warning about Ruth, and a shiver went up my spine. What's this got to do with me?

"If you only knew," Sly said, looking at me with disdain.

"Knew what?" she demanded, still on her knees.

Sly pursed his lips and looked away.

"What?!" she shrieked, yanking on his belt.

Sly hesitated. "I can't tell you what happened in our counseling sessions. It's confidential. Let's just say, all three of these boys are in imminent danger of losing their immortal souls. With the departure of Jimmy, we've already lost one of our recruits, and we can't risk another. The ship of state is hemorrhaging! We must stanch the flow of vital bodily fluids before we sink below the waves!"

"But must it be—Stallion Ranch?" she cried.

"Yes!" Sly said forcefully. "You've got to break the wild mustang to a life of heterosexual domesticity!"

I leaned over to Jackson. "Maybe it's a dude ranch?" I whispered.

Jackson's face brightened. "Cowboys!"

Now nearly blubbering, Ruth clutched Sly's arm. "You'll ruin him!" she sobbed.

"Unhand me, woman!" Sly jerked his arm away and Ruth collapsed on the floor. "Sister, I don't think you realize the peril we are facing with these reprobates. We're not just talking about your ordinary slip, here. We are faced with the prospect of a cataclysmic fall! A plummet! A rapid descent, hurtling downward to the nether reaches of Hell! I realize we're between a rock and a hard place, a bump and a thump. But sometimes you have to fight fire with hellfire to cleanse the body for Christ!"

31: Stallion Ranch

The Rev piled us into the van, and we took off. Perry sat in the front seat next to Sly, and Jackson and I got in the back. Sly gave us no time to pack or take anything with us. "Where we're going, you won't need anything."

Jackson glanced over at me. "Sounds like heaven."

Sly looked over his shoulder. "Now that's the spirit!"

To tell you the truth, I was a little nervous. I'd already guessed what Stallion Ranch was, but when I-80 split in Sacramento and we headed toward Reno, Jackson got it into his head that Sly was going to make men out of us by taking us gambling.

"I don't think so," I said.

"Forget slots," he said. "You might as well throw your money out the window. Black Jack's the best odds, next to odd and even or red and black on the roulette wheel. You have to count the face cards, though now they have a six-deck deal, which makes it harder to keep track. And if they catch you counting, you get rubbed out by the Mafia."

"Jackson," I said, "We're not going gambling."

"We're not?"

"No."

"Where we going?"

Sly piped up just then. It was uncanny how he could track conversations in the back of the van, with all the traffic noise whizzing by. "What's all this cuggermugger going on back there? We're headed to the Boom Boom Room," he announced, "or the Steam and Cream, for you novices."

This confirmed my suspicions. Jackson suddenly got very quiet.

"What's that?" Perry asked.

"We're going to make a gentlemanly call on the Ladies of the Night," Sly said.

Perry still didn't get it. "I don't know any ladies in Nevada."

Jackson kicked the back of his seat. "It's a whorehouse, you diddlebrain."

"What?" he exclaimed. "But I'm a virgin!"

"Ooh," Jackson taunted, "whores just love to gobble up boy virgins!"

"No!" he exclaimed. "This isn't right! I'm saving myself for my future wife!"

The Rev reached over and patted his knee. "Before you're in the least bit capable of satisfying your future wife, you need to be broken in a bit." Then he turned his head to announce, "I want to give you boys a few tips on the Cyprian Arts. These girls are professional sybarites. They know what they're doing, and if you go along with the program, you'll learn a lot tonight about what it takes to give pleasure to a woman. You think Virtual Reality was something—just wait till you try the real thing! And that's exactly what you need. No more pussy-footing around."

Then he explained that when we arrived, they'd show us the girls and we could pick whomever we wanted. "Now listen up. You may be tempted to nab a buxom babe with big boobs, but the older broads can give you delights you never dreamed of." He seemed to relish this thought for a moment, and then continued. "Sassy young tarts may be knock-outs to look at, but believe me, the hussies have been around the corral a few times. They know how to take care of twiddlepoops like you who are shy and awkward around girls. If you nab one of these high-strung fillies, you'd better be ready to reign her in and ride her hard or she'll buck you off in a second. Then you'll never get it up. You understand what I'm saying?"

We nodded, glumly.

"Now don't get too excited," he said. "Keep your lump in your pants. We don't want you to cream your jeans before you even have a chance to take them off."

He chortled at his own joke. At least he was enjoying himself.

*   *   *

When we finally pulled into this dusty parking lot, far off the main highway in he desert outside of Reno, the only lump I had was in my throat. I could not imagine being able to perform for these girls, and resigned myself to a humiliating experience.

It was already late at night. We piled out of the van and stretched our legs after the long drive. Stallion Ranch looked like any motel you'd see along the highway, only on top was a neon sign outlining a cowboy riding a bucking bronco. The air was balmy, with the smell of desert blossoms mixed with diesel fuel from the trucks lined up in the parking lot. Three guys wearing cowboy hats carrying six-packs walked across the crunchy gravel, talking in low voices among themselves. Somehow I'd expected a lot more whooping it up and carrying on.

Jackson elbowed me in the ribs and raised his eyebrows. "Buckaroos!"

Perry said, "It isn't right. It's not part of God's plan. It's against Scripture. It's consorting with Jezebels!"

"Will you just can it with your womanly whining?" Sly said, not terribly sympathetic. "This is the chance of a lifetime to cure yourself of your affliction. Now pull yourself together and take it like a man!"

We walked into this dimly-lit entryway, with tacky velvet paintings of nudes with big breasts glowing under ultra-violet lamps. A hostess greeted us, an older woman I assumed was the Madam of the house. She was dressed in a long, sea-green evening gown, with flowing chiffon sleeves, ropes of pearls, and diamonds the size of rocks on most of her fingers. Her hair was piled on top of her head, and the skin on her face was taut, as though it had been pulled too tight when she brushed back her hair.

She greeted us with a puff on her cigarette, which crackled in a fiery bead at the end of a long holder. "Good evening, Reverend," she said, as if they were old buddies. "How can we help you gentlemen tonight?"

Sly took off his cap. "I thought you might be able to fix up my boys here," he said, rather jovially. Then he leaned over and whispered, "With a few of your girls who have a little patience, if you catch my drift."

She sized us up, smiling. "I think we can handle this gang of rough-riders." Then she clapped her hands, and a bevy of girls came out from behind a curtain, about a dozen blonds, redheads, and brunettes in various forms of drag—a few in shorts with revealing halter tops, about half in bikinis, and the rest in an assortment of uniforms and fetish-like ensembles: a nurse, complete with starched hat, stethoscope and sensible shoes; a black nun; a Chinese policewoman; and a husky dominatrix with a leather bra, miniskirt, motorcycle cap, thrashing a whip.

"Ooh, baby," Jackson nudged me. "That one must be for Sly."

They strutted through the room and took various sultry poses on the couches and chairs in the smoky lounge. The cop stood off to the side, swinging a billy club; the nurse held a giant thermometer, which she shook and stroked; the nun got on her knees and crossed herself; and the dominatrix cracked her whip, then put her foot on the coffee table and rested her forearms on her knee.

"Take your time, boys," the Madam said.

Jackson scratched his chin, and shifted his weight from one foot to the other as he scrutinized the bevy of choices. Perry looked terrorized, and clutched Sly's arm. I felt like I was in a bad movie, and didn't think I could go through with this.

I immediately ruled out all the fetishes. And the girls in bikinis with blond hair and silky skin looked way too intimidating. I gulped and took a big breath, then chose this woman wearing shorts and a halter top who was probably in her mid-thirties. She had medium brown hair and a kind smile, not nearly so coquettish or made up as the other girls. I reached out my hand and she took it, then we headed out back.

"Yo!" Jackson called to me just as we turned the corner. "Dude!"

I looked back and held up my thumb, a smile plastered across my face to hide my trepidation.

32: Like a Virgin

The motel rooms were arranged in a horseshoe around the parking lot. As we walked along the corridor she asked me my name.

"Paul."

"Hi Paul. My name's Diana. Is this your first time?"

I nodded.

"Well that's fine. We'll just have a little fun. There's nothing to worry about."

She let us inside the room, turned on a lamp, and pulled back the covers on the bed. It was just a regular motel room, with a king-size bed, a dresser holding a dish of condoms and a tray of hard liquor. A TV sat on top of a VCR, with a stack of porno tapes next to it. I noticed Lizzie Takes a Lashing, Tarzan Meets Jane, and The Mudslingers Revenge, among others. I looked around like I'd never seen a motel room before.

"Not quite what you expected, is it?"

"Uh, well no. I don't know," I said.

"Make yourself comfortable. I'm going to freshen up a bit."

"Okay." I sat on the bed, and she disappeared inside the bathroom. Just then, someone knocked on the window. I parted the curtain to see Jackson walk by with the Chinese cop. He grinned at me, and I quickly shut the curtain and shuddered.

I figured I could take off now and just hang out by the van until the others finished—no one would be the wiser. But there was a part of me that was also a little intrigued by the prospect of actually making love to a woman, though still doubtful about my ability to pull it off. Plus I didn't want to hurt her feelings.

I wasn't sure if I should get undressed, or if she was supposed to undress me. I decided to take off my shirt, since it was kind of hot, but I kept my pants on.

She came back out wearing a sheer dressing gown with nothing on underneath. I averted my eyes. "It's okay to look, honey. That's what you're here for. Why don't you slip those pants off, I think you'll be a lot more comfortable."

I shyly took off my shoes and pants, but kept my shorts on. She took me by the hand and led me into the bathroom, where she pulled down my shorts and proceeded to wash off my genitals over the sink. She bathed my penis in the warm, soapy water and caressed my balls with a washcloth. Then she pulled back my foreskin, obviously inspecting my penis for sores and lesions. "I always love a foreskin," she said. "They're so much fun to play with, the way they slide back and forth." She proceeded to stroke my penis by sliding the foreskin up and down. "Don't you think so?"

I shrugged. "I don't know. I guess I've always had one."

"You guess?" she said, and laughed.

The slight erection I'd started to get as she stroked me quickly subsided when she laughed.

"Well, that's nothing to worry about," she assured me. "I've always said, 'Soft penises have feelings, too!'"

I nodded, ruefully. Then she dried me off and led me back toward the bed. She let her robe fall off her shoulders and stood before me, stark naked. She touched my chest, and took my hand and placed it on her breast. Then she drew me close to her and kissed me on the lips. She felt soft and smelled perfumy and she tasted good, like peppermint. But nothing was happening.

"Why don't we get a little more comfortable?" she said, and moved us onto the bed. I lay on my back while she ran her hair over my chest and stomach, and then she licked my nipples. She nuzzled my neck, but I raised my shoulder 'cause it tickled.

"Oh!" I squealed, "don't!"

"Ah, you're ticklish," she said. "I'm sorry." Then she blew a raspberry on my stomach and I let out a whoop, laughing.

She leaned on her elbow and smiled at me. "Do you have a girlfriend?"

I shook my head.

"Boyfriend?"

I blushed. Was it that obvious?

"Who's that man who brought you here? Is he really some kind of minister?"

I told her we were ex-gays.

"Oh no," she said, stifling a laugh. "You must be kidding."

"No, it's true."

"What is this? A field trip?"

I nodded.

"Take you boys to a whore, and she's supposed to cure you?"

I shrugged.

She shook her head and grinned. "That's the hokiest thing I ever heard of!"

I turned away from her.

"Oh Paul." She tried to turn me over, but I resisted. She traced my shoulder with her finger. "I'm sorry, Paul, I'm not laughing at you. I'm laughing at the idea that a leopard can change his spots."

I looked over my shoulder. "What do you mean?"

She said, "I hate to be the one to tell you this, but I don't think it works that way."

"You don't?"

"No. It's not your fault you feel the way you do. Why do you want to change?"

"It's not what God wants," I said, cradling my head in the pillow.

"Who told you that?"

"The Reverend. And the Bible."

"Listen to me," she said, and turned me over on my back. I pulled the sheet across my waist. "God made you this way, no one else. Oh sure, you can have fun with a girl, we could even have a roll in the hay if you wanted to, but that doesn't prove a thing. It's what's in your heart that counts."

"Do you really think so?" I asked.

"Yes I do."

"I thought I was supposed to change. God knows, I've been trying to. But no matter what I do, I keep being drawn to other guys."

Diana took my cheeks in her hands and looked me in the eye. "Paul, I want you to promise me one thing."

"What's that?"

"From now on, don't you ever let anyone tell you you're not totally fine just exactly the way you are."

My eyes suddenly filled with tears.

"Oh, honey," she said, and clasped me to her.

I wept in her arms. "I feel like such a total failure," I said, my lips pressed against her breast.

"It's okay," she said, stroking my hair. "You're not a failure. Not at all. They're just trying to get you to be something that's not in your true nature."

"And I—I let Jimmy go!"

"Is Jimmy your boyfriend?"

"Well I w-wish he was!" I sobbed. "But he went away. I practically drove him away! Even though he said he really c-cared for me," I hiccupped. "And then—then I came here!"

"You should go after him, then. Tell him you love him—that's what's important. Never mind the rest. And I hate to say it, since who am I to talk, but that Reverend of yours is wrong. Dead wrong."

She held me while I cried some more, rocking me in her arms. I felt warm and safe, and comforted for the first time in a long, long while.

* * *

Sly winked at me when I came into the lobby, no doubt assuming I'd finally gotten laid. I'm sure I must have looked much calmer. Jackson soon joined us, and strutted through the parking lot like the cock of the walk.

"Dude!" Jackson crowed. "It was hot! Bodacious! A most excellent adventure!"

I couldn't tell whether he was really as thrilled as he claimed he was. I suspected he was putting on a show for Sly. Perry slunk into the van and seemed practically catatonic for the entire ride home—definitely not a happy camper. I didn't say much, either.

In any event, Sly seemed pleased and confident with his judgment that going to the whorehouse was the bee's knees in terms of finally getting us over the hump of our sexual brokenness. "At last you boys have gotten a taste of what you're missing," he said as we pulled out of the parking lot. "Now that you've sown your wild oats, what you want to do is find a nice Christian girl and settle down to a life of domestic tranquility."

To prevent the possibility of a serious relapse, Sly decided to move up the schedule. He set a date for me to marry Ruth.

33: Somebody's Gotta Do It

When I awoke the next day, it was very bright outside. Birds were whistling and squeaking in the trees. I felt sticky and hot. I turned over on my back and stared at the ceiling, trying to remember the night's events and sort out which ones really happened and which ones were only a dream.

We got back to Escape at dawn. I crawled into my bunk, comforted by the familiar musty smell of the pine cabin, and fell into a deep sleep. I dreamt first I was with Diana; then Jimmy joined us and Diana danced and leapt about the room while Jimmy and I made love.

Then I gulped at the thought of marrying Ruth. I couldn't quite picture a life of domestic tranquility with her. I remembered Diana's warning that I must follow my true nature, whatever that might be. And the medium's prediction that false friends would lead me astray from my true goal. The Devil came in so many guises, it seemed almost impossible to tell what was true and what was false.

I looked around the cabin, but everyone else had long since gotten up. I decided I'd better talk to the Rev about this wedding idea at our counseling session. Although Ruth was younger than Sly, she was still nearly twenty years older than me. I admit, she often took a special interest in me during Bible study, when you consider my ignorance of most Scriptural matters. And she seemed like a nice enough person, but as far as I was concerned, there was nothing like romance going on between us.

I knocked at Sly's office. There wasn't any answer, so I tried the door. Sly was seated at his desk, watching TV. He reached for the remote on his

VCR, but it slipped out of his hand and skidded across the floor. He was watching a gay porn video. I picked up the remote.

"Oh, hi, Paul," he said. "Is Bible study over? I was just reviewing some more of these obscene videos for my testimony before the Select Senate Committee on Pornography. See, I take notes." He indicated the notebook that covered his lap, while various studs pumped away in a steamy orgy on the screen.

"You have to keep up with the Devil. It's a hellish job," he joked, "but somebody's gotta do it." Then he continued in his usual obscure language: "Of course, coprology—the study of dirty pictures—does not necessarily reflect grapholagnia—an intense interest in obscenity. It's all in the service of hamartiology—the study of sin."

"If this isn't a good time—" I said.

"No problemo! Unless you wanted to help me review this sinful smut." He chuckled.

I must have curled my lip, because he immediately rescinded the offer. "No, on second thought, it would probably be overstimulating, and we wouldn't want to put your recovery in jeopardy, now would we?"

I shook my head. Sly took the remote from me and shut off the video. "So what can we do for you this bright and sunny morning?"

"Well, I thought this was our regular meeting time."

He glanced at his watch. "So it is! Amazing how one loses track of time when one is deeply engrossed in one's work. Have a seat, Paul, and tell me about your rousing success last night with—what's her name?"

"Diana."

"Diana, the huntress. Rowr, rowr!" he growled. "Bet she showed you a few tricks." He gave me his sly grin.

"Um well—"

"Paul, I can't tell you how proud I am. In the short time since you joined Escape, you've made excellent progress towards a heterosexual adjustment. Perhaps a few temptations here and there, but that's par for the course."

"But I really don't think I'm ready to get married."

"Nonsense! You're ready as you'll ever be. Best thing for you, quite frankly. You have just gotten the merest taste of the pleasures that await you. But for you it's an acquired taste, which marriage will reinforce."

I tried to bring up my hesitation about Ruth, but he waved off my objections.

"Marriage is a beautiful, sacred thing: to berth yourself at the dock of matrimonial bliss, a safe harbor against temptation, the wild tempestuous seas of unnatural lust that churn and agitate the soul. It's a rock and an anchor! A haven and a blessing." Sly stared out the window, looking wistful.

"Well," I said, "I guess I'd better get on to Bible study."

"It's always a pleasure to see you, Paul. Give my regards to the others. I'm sure Ruth is looking forward to seeing you, too."

I nodded and quietly closed the door behind me. Walking back outside, I kicked myself. For some reason I couldn't tell him I wasn't going to marry Ruth. I began to wonder if he was right: I just needed to give it a try, then I wouldn't be tempted anymore. But with Ruth? Oh, God, the very thought made me shrivel. If I couldn't get it on with Diana there was no way in hell I could ever get it up for Ruth. As if I even wanted to!

Walking toward the Fireside Room, I was broken out of my reverie by a voice behind me. "Yo! Dude!"

I looked over my shoulder. "Jimmy!"

He caught up with me and clapped me on the back. "Hey Paul, what's happening?"

I was totally shocked. I never thought I'd see him again, and here he was, standing right in front of me, cute as the devil. "When did you get back?"

"This morning. Everyone was still asleep, so I took a walk. Is Sly letting you guys carouse around, or what?"

"Well not exactly." I hesitated telling him about the whorehouse. It just seemed too complicated. "So, what are you doing here?" I asked.

"I've come to take you away from all this," he said, spreading his arms, indicating the ranch.

Suddenly that old familiar yearning rose again in my heart. As we walked toward the cabin, my mind was all in a whir: incredibly tempted, but as usual, confused. To go from thinking marriage might cure me to Jimmy showing up and saying he still wanted me was a little overwhelming. I couldn't think of anything to say.

"I realized it was stupid to lay some trip on you at the conference," he continued. "I really like you, but I can't see the point as long as you're trapped in this cult."

"Cult?" I said, somewhat defensively. "It's not really a cult. No one's keeping us from leaving."

"Then come with me."

"Uh, well, I don't think I'm ready to leave quite yet." How weird it was—only last night, I'd felt such sorrow at letting him go, such despair at never seeing him again. Yet here he was, offering to take me with him, and I was feeling shy and uncertain. As much as I wanted him, I mistrusted my own desires.

We entered the bunkhouse. "Look, I'm not asking you to marry me," he said, as if he could read my mind. "Not like Ruth, anyway," he said, obviously rubbing it in.

My heart sank again at the thought of Ruth. Suddenly the thought of staying was mixed with as much foreboding as leaving. "I guess I just still have some stuff I need to work out," I said, standing in the doorway.

"Like what?"

"Well, whether I'm even capable of being normal, for one thing." I thought of my encounter with Diana, who assured me that I could be exactly what I am without apologies to anyone. And yet I loved her, in a way. Or I was at least grateful to her, and felt comforted by her. Whereas around Jimmy, I felt acutely uncomfortable.

"What's 'normal'?"

I entered the room and sat on my bunk. "I don't know. Maybe 'normal' is getting up in the morning and kissing your wife and seeing the kids off to school and having someone to come home to at night who isn't drunk or drugged out, or lashing out at you because you remind him of being queer all the time."

Jimmy sat next to me and put his arm around my shoulder. "You really are a sick puppy," he said.

"Maybe I am." I turned towards him. "So why are you so interested in me? Will you score points with your Homo Nation friends if you seduce me?"

He let his arm drop. He rested his forearms on his knees, looking wounded. For a second I relented. Why was I pushing him away, when I had so yearned for him the night before?

Then he hit his knee and launched into this tirade: "I can't stand these self-righteous bigots who try to force their religious hatred on everyone else!"

"Sly's not like that," I said. "He's just trying to help gays who feel unhappy."

"That slimy hypocrite! He wanted me to pose naked for his laser scan."

So it was true! The same body I'd made love to in Virtual Reality, Sly had seen in the flesh. And of course Sly had come on to me in his own weird way, to say nothing of his porn videos.

"If you hate him so much, why did you agree to pose for him?" I asked, realizing with a twinge I was actually jealous.

"'Cause I knew you'd see it," he said, and smirked. I blushed.

Then he said, "You really have to question the motivation of so-called counselors who flash pictures of naked men and then jolt you with an electric shock when you get a hard-on. To say nothing of trying to seduce you."

God, was Sly coming on to everyone?

"And why do you think you're unhappy? What is it you believe about being gay that's making you so unhappy?"

"It's in the Bible," I said, weakly.

"All that Bible thumping is nothing but spiritual abuse. The Bible supports slavery, too, but no one quotes the Bible to defend slavery anymore."

That's true. I'd never thought of it that way.

"The only people who think gays can change are the ones who think they should change. Anyone who doesn't have a vested interest in us being straight can look at the evidence and see that same-sex attraction doesn't just go away. Escape is a cult—"

"Wait a minute. What about all those testimonials from ex-gays at Homo-Anon meetings?"

"Come on. Sly twisted your arm to give a testimonial yourself at the ex-gay convention. Are you cured?"

"Well, I was trying," I said. "That counts for something."

"You should have seen all these 'ex-gays' out cruising each other in the restrooms at the Anaheim Convention Center!"

Given my history, I was surprised I'd missed that.

"Paul! It's so obvious. Anyone who seeks a cure through religious conversion is only doing do so because of internalized homophobia."

"But what about all the self-loathing, the drugs, the alcohol, the unsafe sex?"

"If we really accepted ourselves," he said, "we could just love each other instead of trying to escape from our feelings."

I felt myself weakening, running out of arguments.

"Anyone can suppress their behavior," Jimmy said. "But can you honestly say you don't think about guys anymore?"

I looked away, unable to face him.

He took me by the shoulders and turned me toward him. I avoided his glance, but he kept peering at me until I finally met his sparking eyes. I gazed at his face, his wine-colored lips, felt his hands squeeze my shoulders, and my penis jumped.

He leaned forward, moving closer until his lips grazed mine. This time I didn't pull away, and he kissed me. His lips were soft and moist, his tongue gently probing, intertwined with mine. He pulled me close to his chest and my arms reached around his back. I closed my eyes and felt myself melt into his embrace. Then he breathed in my ear, "I love you, Paul," sending chills up my spine.

Just then, Sly burst into the cabin, pointing at Jimmy. "Ah ha! So there you are, you renegade apostate!"

I instinctively pulled away, looking guiltily at Sly.

"Well, speak of the Devil," Jimmy said.

34: Beat the Devil

"You depraved, perverted debaucher!" Sly shouted at Jimmy. "I want you off this property!"

"Hold onto your shorts, Sly."

"Right this instant! Or I'm calling the police!"

Jimmy ignored him and turned to me. "Why don't you get your stuff together and we'll meet out front."

"He's not going anywhere!" Sly countered.

"What?" said Jimmy. "You're holding him against his will?"

"Unlike you," Sly said, "Paul made a commitment to finish this program."

"Come hell or high water, I suppose."

"Don't you talk to me about hell, you arch fiend seducer, Prince of Darkness, heathenish homo pagan!" Sly said. "You're going to burn for eternity! Now get out!"

Jimmy gave me a quick kiss. "I'll meet you out front. We can catch a bus into town."

I watched him as he left the cabin and strode across the lawn. My lips burned. Only one thought seared my brain: I can't let him walk away from me again! I knew I was risking my soul in eternity, but hell couldn't be any worse than what I was putting myself through now. I decided I would just go to hell, and started to pack my stuff.

But Sly grabbed me by the arm. "You violated the no-contact rule."

"You're hurting my arm."

"A lot more than that will be hurting if I allow you to descend into the depths of depravity. Lucky for you Ruth spied Jimmy across the lawn, luring you into his web of lies and Satanic intrigue!"

"Let me go!"

Sly dragged me out of the cabin and across the quad to his office. He shoved me inside and slammed the door. "First Peter 3:14 tells us, 'Even if you suffer for righteousness' sake, you will be blessed.'"

Then he pulled some boxing gloves out of the closet that had the pin-up girl from his club in Saigon. He threw the gloves on the desk and took off his shirt.

"Strip," he commanded.

I hesitated.

"I said, 'Strip!'" He reached over and ripped the shirt right off my back. My buttons went flying. Sly stripped down to his underwear and put on a devil's mask: it had a thin face painted purple and scarlet, with narrow slits for eyes, pointed ears, a goatee, and horns. Then he pulled on his boxing gloves.

"Put on your gloves!"

"Sly, I don't want to do this. Let's just call it quits, okay?"

"No, it's not 'okay,'" he said through his mask in a faggy imitation of my plea. "Just because you're so weak-willed you're ready to chuck everything I've prepared you for, I'm not going to let you succumb to temptation without a fight!"

"I don't want to fight. I'm tired of fighting it."

Sly reached out and batted my chest. "Come on, put up your dukes. Counter temptation with masculine energy. Don't give in. Beat the Devil!"

I reluctantly put on the gloves. I was obviously totally outmatched, and resigned myself to taking a beating.

He sparred with me, dancing around the office, jabbing at my shoulder. "Hold up your guard!"

I held my gloves in front of me, and he feinted at my forearm and then punched me in the ribs. I backed off, trying to avoid his punches, occasionally deflecting one with my left glove.

"Thataboy," he said, then he moved in tighter and punched me a couple of times in the face, knocking me over. I sprawled across the floor.

"Get up, you lubber!" He kicked me in the butt. "Don't be such a pansy. Don't be a wimp!"

I got up reeling, barely able to catch my balance again, when he punched me in the stomach, knocking the breath out of me.

"Come on! Don't be a whuss! Show us a little fight! Give us some spunk!"

I got mad, finally, and started to spar with him. I tried to get in a couple of jabs, which he knocked to the side. "That's better! Give us a little competition. Send us packing. Wrestle with Satan!"

I landed a punch on his chest.

"That's the spirit! Fight off those demons! Battle with Beelzebub!"

Then I got into it. I fended off his uppercut and lunged in to pummel his chest. He crossed his forearms, laughing. I battered his defenses, then delivered a powerful blow to his stomach. "Oomph!" he cried, doubling over. His mask slipped, so he couldn't see, and I finished him off with a coup de grace to the chin. He went hurtling backwards and crashed against the wall. His framed certificate from the Universal Life Church fell off and knocked him on the noggin, then crashed, shattering glass across the floor.

I pulled off the gloves, grabbed my shirt and dashed out of the office. I ran outside, at first intending to go back to the cabin for my stuff, then decided to hell with it. It was now or never—who knew if Jimmy was even still waiting for me?

So I high-tailed it for the road, when suddenly I ran into Jackson, completely out of breath and looking stricken. "Paul! Quick! We got to find Perry! He's gonna kill himself!"

35: Sex, Lies, and Porno

Jackson shoved a page of lined notebook paper in my face. On it was neatly printed an obvious suicide note:

Dear Fellow Escapees,

I know God will forgive me for what I'm about to do, but God could never forgive me for indulging another homosexual thought, word, or deed: 'Verily I say unto you, the wages of sin is death'—Romans 6:23. Yet Romans 6:7 assures us, 'He that is dead is freed from sin.'

With this act, I am saving myself from a fate worse than death—at least in death I will be united with our Lord and Savior, sweet Jesus.

Thank you all for your kind help. I only apologize for your misplaced confidence in me.

Yours in Christ, Perry.

"Oh, fuck!" I cried. "Where did you find this? Where is he? Where are the others?"

"I don't know where he is! Ruth canceled Bible study and I just found this note on Perry's bed."

We ran back to the Fireside Room and drafted Sheila to help look for him. We fanned out over the compound and searched all the buildings. Jackson and Sheila took the barn theater and farmhouse. I ran back to the cabin and looked around the bunks, then entered the bathroom. "Perry?" I checked the stalls and peeked inside the shower, afraid of what I might find—but it was empty. When I turned to go back through the cabin, there was Ruth, blocking the door. "Ruth! Have you seen Perry?"

She took off her glasses and shook her head. Her hair came loose and cascaded over her shoulders. The top of her blouse was unbuttoned.

Under normal circumstances, I would have thought it was odd to find Ruth standing in the doorway of the boys' bathroom, wearing ruby lipstick, letting her hair down. I was dimly aware that something was wrong with this picture, but I was so preoccupied with finding Perry before something awful happened that my unease with her display only hovered at the edge of my mind like a vague premonition.

She twirled her finger through a spiral of hair. "Tell me, Paul, am I as tempting as that Jezebel you consorted with last night?"

"What?" It took me a moment to register what she was talking about.

"That whore of Babylon," she added, with a tight growl. Then she lifted her chin at an angle, exposing the nape of her neck, and batted her eyes. Without her glasses, she seemed to be peering at someone over my shoulder.

Of course she meant Diana, but I decided I should keep any comparisons to myself. "Oh sure, Ruth, you look swell, but we've got to find Perry! We found this note." I held it out to her.

"Don't patronize me, Paul. I couldn't stand it if you scorned me."

"Ruth! Look. This is really serious. Perry's trying to commit suicide!" I tried to move through the doorway, but she pressed against me, the smell of gin on her breath. "Oh Jesus," I mumbled.

"The Reverend told me he set our wedding date," she said, addressing my nipple.

"Uh, yes, I've been meaning to talk to you," I said, pulling my shirt together while I tried to squeeze past her. "But right now I think we'd better find Perry before he kills himself!" I wrenched free and rushed out of the cabin to join Jackson and Sheila in the quad. "Any sign of him?" I asked.

"No," said Sheila. "We looked all through the house and the theater."

"The treatment room!" Jackson suggested. We hustled over to the office building and ran down the corridor to the screening room.

It was locked. "Perry!" we shouted and banged on the door. I shoved my shoulder against the door, but it wouldn't budge. "Rats!"

We ran outside and Jackson boosted me up to the window. I pushed up the sash and broke through the black-out paper that had been used to darken the room. Sitting in the recliner with the wire from the plethysmograph looped around his neck, was Perry.

I ripped off the rest of the black paper to let in the light, fearing the worst. He had obviously tried to electrocute himself. "Perry!" I cried.

He turned and looked at me, squinting at my silhouette against the light. "Paul?"

"Yes!"

Jackson groaned under my weight. "Is he all right?"

"I think so. Perry, open the door!"

He got up and reached for the door, but the wire pulled on his neck. "No! Wait! Just sit still." I climbed through the window, while Jackson and Sheila raced around to the door. "Take it easy," I said. I turned off the peter meter and carefully loosened the wire and lifted it over his head. Jackson and Sheila pounded on the door and I let them in.

"You fool!" shouted Jackson. "What the hell's the matter with you, anyway!"

"Leave him alone," I said. "At least he's safe."

"I don't think any of us is safe around here," Sheila said.

"That goes for me, too," Jackson said. "This place is a nut house."

"What happened last night, anyway?" Sheila asked.

Perry looked sort of sheepish. "It wasn't just last night, although going to the ranch confirmed it for me. I remembered what the Rev told us: 'If you haven't been delivered over to heterosexuality, it's because your motivation isn't strong enough. If you still have homosexual feelings, you're not doing enough meetings, Bible study, prayer, or fellowshipping.' I kept experiencing more guilt and self-loathing, and repented again and again for my lustful thoughts.

"I already felt like taking a gun to my head, when we went to the whorehouse and this foxy lady told me I was a limp fish. Finally I couldn't repent anymore—I just didn't have the strength. I figured Sly was right—I was better off dead than returning to a life of sin and degradation. This seemed like a fitting end to my misery." He held up the wire attached to the plethysmograph.

He went on to tell us he was afraid he'd caused Sly's "fall." The night they shared a room with Jackson at the ex-gay convention, there were only two double beds. "I slept with the Rev, and we had sex," he sobbed, tears streaming down his face.

"That bastard," Sheila said.

"It wasn't the Reverend's fault!" Perry wailed. "I wanted it to happen. I guess I'm so wicked that I could even cause a man of the cloth to burn in lust and fall into sexual brokenness."

"It all don't be on you," Jackson said. Then it came out that Sly had tried to seduce all the guys, each with some line about healing our sexual brokenness by merging our masculine energies.

"Then I found this tape in Sly's office," Perry said, holding up a videocassette. He slipped the tape into the VCR. We watched the TV in amazement as it showed Sly going down on Perry. "This was during our 'Deep Tissue Realignment Therapy' after we got back from the convention." Perry covered his face in shame.

"He was taping you?" Sheila asked.

"He taped all of us during Aversive Therapy." He rewound the tape. We saw quick clips of Perry, Jackson, and then me sitting in the screening room, each of us getting hard-ons in response to the slides of naked guys. "Every time Sly left the room, he was watching us on a monitor. Plus he has a hidden camera in his office."

Jackson said, "What a lewdster."

"This is totally bizarre," Sheila said. "Let's show this tape to Ruth."

I was about to explain that Ruth had her own problems, when a voice behind us said, "That won't be necessary." We whirled around to discover Ruth standing in the doorway, holding a pistol. "I've already seen it."

36: Ye Shall Be as Gods

"Ruth!" Sheila said. "What are you doing?"

"Just as there will be a reckoning in heaven to come, so shall there be a reckoning on earth for scoffers, heretics, and unbelievers." Since our encounter in the men's room, Ruth had rebuttoned her blouse and put on her glasses. Her hair still hung down to her shoulders. She confiscated the tape and took us at gun-point down the hall to Sly's office.

Sly, dressed again in his camouflage fatigues and clerical collar, took the gun and the incriminating videotape. "Thank you, sister," he said. "We don't want to support the porno industry, do we? It's far better to use our own material for desensitizing ex-gays."

"That is such bullshit," Sheila said. "You're nothing but a humbug, a charlatan, and a pervert."

"How dast thou condemn me with your calumny?" Sly said, indignantly. "I am a Pastor of Life, a Physician of the Soul. I've taken the Hypocritic Oath!"

I couldn't help but snicker at his obvious slip.

He narrowed his eyes at me and lifted his chin. "Having passed through my own struggle with homopathology, I became acquainted with the Lord through the grace of the Holy Ghost in relationship to my acts of repentance. Since learning to abide in Jesus, I discovered a natural bent for integrating theology with the treatment of sexual brokenness. Proverbs 11:14 advises us, 'Where no Counselor is, the people fall.' Others may scoff, but those are my qualifications."

"It's not a question of scoffing, you scumbag," Sheila said. "Perry just tried to kill himself because you molested him!"

"Just like you tried to seduce the rest of us," Jackson added.

Sly let out a howl like a wounded animal. "Sirrah! What is all this humdudgeon? Am I solely responsible for the sins of the world? Did I force myself on any of you? Is there no free will? No forgiveness of sins?"

"So what's your game plan?" I asked. "If you can't convert us or seduce us, you'll just get rid of us?"

"I'm surprised at you," Sly said. "What did you think this was, Jonestown? Or Waco, Texas?"

It crossed my mind, but I kept my mouth shut.

Then Sly raised the gun in benediction and recited from the Bible: "'Come now, let us reason together. Blessed are you when men revile you and persecute you and utter all kinds of evil against you falsely on my account.' Then he looked at us sternly and said, "'He that is not for me is against me.'"

Ruth put her hand inside my elbow. "I was promised in marriage to you," she said, "and I intend to keep our appointment with Destiny. If the good Reverend would please perform the ceremony."

"I would be happy to."

I said, "Not a chance!"

Suddenly Sly grabbed Perry and pointed the gun at his head. Perry squealed. "Shut up, you little pig," Sly commanded. Sly held Perry in a headlock while Ruth put a sash around Sly's neck. She picked up a gilt-edged Bible and held it in her hands.

Perry whimpered. Sheila leaned over to me and whispered, "Maybe we should just go along with this charade."

Sheila was right, we should put up with one last farce just to save our skins. Only I wasn't convinced this ceremony would be the last rite we were forced to participate in. What was next? More naked laser scans? Ritualized sacrifices? Virtual orgies?

"Dearly Beloved, we are gathered here in the sight of God and Man to celebrate the Sacrament of Holy Matrimony. 'What therefore God hath joined together, let no man break asunder.'" As the Rev droned on through the liturgy, I steeled myself for a fate worse than death. "Do you, Ruth Slocock, take Paul to be your lawfully wedded husband, to honor and obey—"

"Yes yes yes!" Ruth said, obviously impatient. "I do."

"And do you, Paul, take Ruth to be your lawfully wedded wife, to have and to hold, to love and to cherish, in sickness and in health, as long as you both shall live?"

I thought, just say it and be done with it and get the hell out of here. Ruth turned to me, her eyes closed, her lips puckered, and my will failed me. I couldn't do it. Not for her, not for Perry, not even for the promise of a heterosexual marriage. I couldn't stand the thought of betraying my love for Jimmy.

"No way!" I shouted, and knocked the gun out of Sly's hand. Jackson dove for the gun, but it slid across the floor. Perry elbowed Sly in the stomach and wriggled free from his headlock. Ruth screeched and started beating me over the head with her Bible. Sheila stood between the gun and Sly, who approached her menacingly. "Hi, ya!" she yelled, whirled in the air, and gave Sly a karate kick to the chest. He sprawled backward across his desk. Perry pounced on Ruth and pinned her.

Jackson grabbed the gun and pointed it at Sly. "Yo!" he shouted. "Dude!" Sly held up his hands.

Just then, Jimmy broke through the door with a couple of cops. "Freeze!" Everyone froze.

"Arrest these punks!" Sly demanded. "They ruthlessly attacked a man of the cloth! Beat a defenseless woman senseless!" Ruth, with Perry sitting on her stomach, looked around, obviously in a daze.

But the cops put handcuffs on Sly and Ruth. It turned out they'd had an eye on them both for molesting underage clients while running their pyramid scam with their phony water filters. I recognized one of them as the guy who bought all those filters from Jackson at the street fair. When I failed to come out to the road, Jimmy figured something had gone wrong and went to get help.

Amidst protests of innocence, the police read them their rights and confiscated the guns, tapes, and bogus water filters. When they dragged Sly and Ruth outside to the squad car, Sly condemned us with another slew of Bible quotes, spittle flying from his rabid curses:

"'O, Jerusalem, Jerusalem, killing the prophets and stoning those who are sent to you! Do not throw pearls before swine, lest they trample them underfoot and turn to attack you. Woe unto you, scribes and Pharisees! Ye serpents, ye generation of vipers, how can ye escape the damnation of hell?'"

As the police loaded Sly into the squad car, Sly kept bobbing up and thrusting his head out the door, protesting his innocence, raving over and over, "'Lord, Lord, why hast thou forsaken me?'" The cop finally had to grasp the top of his head and shove him back inside the car. Ruth remained strangely quiet during the entire arrest, but gave me a murderous look as they stuffed her into the back seat with Sly.

The Inspector told us they'd be back later for the Virtual Reality machine. "No!" Sly bellowed, banging his head against the window. "You can't take my VR! It's my pride and joy! More real than reality! 'Ye shall be as gods!' As gods!" he cried, as they hauled them off to jail.

37: Dos Equis

Jimmy called some friends in San Francisco, who came and picked us up later that night. All four of us stayed at his flat on Church Street until we got back on our feet. It was a little crazy at first, as we sprawled in sleeping bags and blankets throughout the apartment. But his roomates were pretty good sports, and every night was like a big slumber party, telling tales about our experiences to Jimmy and his friends from Homo Nation. Jimmy said, "Since you escaped from Escape, what does that make you? Ex-ex-gays?"

"Yeah!" Jackson said, snapping his fingers. "Dos Equis!"

Sly got thrown out of the ex-gay movement, of course, but only because he carried out his duties with too much enthusiasm, not because they've quit trying to convert homosexuals. We had to shake our heads when all these ex-gay ministries started taking out full-page ads with their vivid testimonials claiming gays can change. It's sad to think a whole other generation of vulnerable gays will be led down the path of self-hatred and repressed sexuality.

Sly was charged with having sex with an underaged client, and both he and Ruth were indicted for involuntary imprisonment and reckless endangerment, plus fraud for running the water filter scam.

Sheila gave up trying to look femme—no more dresses, make-up, or high-heeled shoes. "Not that there's anything wrong with lipstick lesbians; it's just not me," she said. She got a job teaching self-defense classes for women.

Jackson hasn't been doing much drag—he said he did it mostly to work his parents' nerves, anyway. Since our falling out with Sly, of course, he lost his whole pyramid of water filter sales, but he's already hustling up a new gig selling sports equipment.

Perry's staying with us—he's almost seventeen, and he really doesn't want to go back to his fundamentalist parents who shipped him off in the first place. He got involved with a youth group sponsored by a church that says you can be gay and Christian, too. They claim all those abominations in the Bible don't really refer to gay relationships, and the early church apparently blessed same-sex unions. I'm glad he's found a way to reconcile his faith with his sexual orientation, but to tell you the truth, I'm kind of over it.

As for me, I decided to get my GED and take some Gay Studies classes at City College. I can't believe they actually have classes at a real college where you can learn about gays in history, art, film, and literature—not that I'd expect to earn a living at it. Who knows, maybe I'll even try to write some of this down. No one would ever believe it, otherwise.

The day after we left the ranch, Jimmy and I went back with a friend's truck to pick up the Virtual Reality machine before the cops had a chance to confiscate it; they already got the tapes, after all. One wall is now lined with computers and the rocket ship takes up half the dining room. We've had fun laser-scanning all our friends, and plan to re-program heaven and hell more to our liking.

I finally contacted my mom, and she's met Jimmy. He thinks it's "way cool" she's still a radical after all these years, when everyone else is out to make a buck (she has a tendency to color her history to conform to whatever she's into at the moment). Still, compared to his own stick-in-the-mud parents, who still can't accept him, she must seem rather refreshing. Jimmy and my mom are always getting into these long involved discussions about feminism, censorship, and civil rights for gay people. I don't say a whole lot, but they still like to give me a hard time for my retro tendencies.

Mom, of course, thought I was a total dope for joining up with Escape in the first place, which is hard to argue, but we seem to get along better now that I'm living on my own. Or I should say, with Jimmy. When Sheila and Jackson found another flat with some friends, Jimmy asked me to stay on with him. I said, "So does that mean we're like, boyfriends?"

He smiled. "If you're sure that's what you want."

I put both hands on his shoulders. "Yup," I said, and kissed him. "That's exactly what I want."

* * *

While still at the ranch, we gave the cops our statements and then waited for Jimmy's friends to pick us up. Perry and Jackson hung out with Sheila in the Fireside Room, while Jimmy and I went back to the bunkhouse. It was just him and me, for the first time since the convention, but this time without the threat of hell hanging over our heads.

In some ways, of course, fire and brimstone added a passionate charge to our contact. I have to admit, I was a little nervous about whether our attraction would outlast the thrill of the forbidden. But I soon discovered there was nothing to worry about. As a matter of fact, I've never felt so free and yet so connected in all my life.

We entered the cabin, holding hands, and pushed our bunks together. The sun cast shadows of leaves across the bed, and a fragrant breeze from the bay laurel floated through the cabin. We hugged, warmly, clasping each other to our chests. Then he took my face in his hands, gazing into my eyes, and we kissed for the first time without fear someone would burst in on us or yank us away from each other.

We took off our shirts and explored our bodies, squeezing the muscles in our chests and arms, stroking our backs and kissing each other's nipples, finally dropping our pants and tumbling onto the bed. Then we hugged and kissed some more, stroking our thighs, feeling one another bulge beneath our underwear, finally pulling off our shorts and reveling in the touch of our penises rubbing and swelling against each other.

Jimmy just happened to have some condoms with him. "You devil," I said. He put the flat circle on his tongue and went down on me. I laughed, running my hands through his hair, and before I knew it I was securely wrapped. We wrestled and hugged and caressed each other, kissing and laughing all through the late afternoon, into the twilight, making love again and again in the full delight of all our senses.

The End

Also by Rik Isensee

Love Between Men—Enhancing Intimacy and Keeping Your Relationship Alive

Reclaiming Your Life—The Gay Man's Guide to Love, Self-Acceptance, and Trust

Are You Ready? The Gay Man's Guide to Thriving at Midlife

	DATE DUE		
JUL 2 6 2008			

Fiction I786 .G577 2000
Isensee, Rik
The God Squad

Printed in the United States
3867

9 780595 006779